NEVER WALK ALONE

NEVER WALK ALONE

RUFUS KING

WILDSIDE PRESS

Also published as *The Case of the Dowager's Etchings*.

Published by Wildside Press LLC
www.wildsidepress.com

CHAPTER 1

The etching was small in size and depicted a stag who, at eventide, had stepped down to a forest pool for a drink. There was a certain charm: a peaceful quality devoid of the usual animal alarms of that nineteenth-century genre in American art when the common practice was to freeze all stags at bay. Unhappily, there was very little of true genius to commend it.

Mrs. Giles did not like to linger too conspicuously before the etching, even though the sight of it hanging on a wall for public exhibition stripped her of five decades and hastened disturbingly the tempo of her heart.

She was a tall woman and still held a willowy effect in her seventieth year; an effect which during her youth had invariably caused her to be compared with the abstract and slightly consumptive-looking women made fashionable by the paintings of Dante Gabriel Rossetti. All through her life this willow quality had surrounded her with a paradox, for Mrs. Giles in reality enjoyed the physical stamina of an amazon.

She saw Dawn Davis, the society columnist of the town's Bridgehaven *Gazette*, bearing toward her through the crush. She decided, from her hat, that Miss Davis had been on a looting expedition in New York. It was the type of hat that Mrs. Giles had often wondered about, while knowing perfectly well it would never go with the silver pompadour and soft-coiled bun to which, through the maelstrom of fashions, she had continued to cling. Apart from everything else, the hat would never stick.

"Surely *you* aren't here, Mrs. Giles," Miss Davis said. "It's the millennium."

Dawn Davis had a husky, almost masculine voice from what some snipers attributed to chain martini drinking. She capitalized on a hale and direct attack. She swiftly noted for her column, "Town Tid-Bits," Carrie Giles's conservatively dripping dark foulards, the white glace kid gloves, the Baba-au-Rhum straw hat with its dash of velvet violets, and the museum-piece brooch-watch of emeralds and gold.

Mentally she niched Carrie Giles among Madame Tussaud's waxworks (English Nobility Groups), although her next morning's column would say: "Among the Sunday crush of Bridgehaven's heavily overflowing defense-plant workers and the town's younger-matron set it was a breath from the world's golden age to come upon the aristocratic Mrs. Chatterton Giles. Rarely during recent years has Mrs. Giles left the shelter of her magnificent estate, River Rest, on the outskirts of Bridgehaven: a house which still predominantly stands out as a bastion for formality and elegance in a society now so attenuated that it might be called dead. Nothing but…"

What *had* brought the old dame out of her gold-plated and shadow-boxed warren today anyhow? Miss Davis wondered. Buying war bonds via this public sale of contributed *objets d'art* (Miss Davis cast a hasty look around the walls and shuddered) could hardly have done it. The Carrie Gileses still left in this world handled their patriotism and their charities privately, as everything they had done all their lives had been private, with a distaste amounting to nausea at any publicity.

"What did bring you here?" Miss Davis asked directly.

"My grandson, I think."

"Kent? But I thought he was overseas."

"He is, Miss Davis. In a sense."

Dawn Davis had a nose beyond teatime chitchat. She scented Front Page.

"Would you mind telling me what you mean by that?"

"I think I am glad to. I have heard there is nothing new left to learn when you are seventy. I am speaking of human relationships, Miss Davis, and not of the whisking contraptions in metal and plastics which astound us so freshly each day. I refer to a code of living."

"And you've learned something new?"

"Yes. It is not enough to give material things. You must also give a part of yourself. Of your heart. I say this with sincere humility and with considerable diffidence, because I doubt whether anyone might any longer find a share in me attractive."

Miss Davis dispersed the swift vision of a Carrie Giles disjointed, and batted platitudes aside. She wanted news.

"I still don't see what this has to do with Kent."

"I am somewhat vague on the point myself, although I feel instinctively that I am right." Mrs. Giles's fine gray eyes clouded. "I have felt wretched. Increasingly wretched."

"Why?"

"The pleasantness, the comfort, the security of my home, Miss Davis. The food on my table. The assurance that I will have the sustenance of three meals a day and will sleep in a comfortable bed every night."

"And Kent can't?"

"No, it both is and it isn't Kent. I think I express myself badly. It is the spirit he serves rather than himself. Kent is a soldier from a long line of soldiers. When I vision him in his fighting plane, the honor and the duty and the glory are all his. They would remain his even though his plane should fall. To take with him always." Mrs. Giles swept a willowy look over the crush. "This is more what I mean."

It still failed to make sense.

"These defense workers?"

"They and the others. All the people who fight without arms. They have no glory to take into death with them. Only discomfort and torment."

"But these lads and lassies—have you any idea how much they are pulling down per week, Mrs. Giles?"

"Does it matter? I understand from your own paper, Miss Davis, that local housing conditions are so critical that many of these workers are crowded into trailers and tents and hovels, and that those who are fortunate enough to get rooms are being charged a shocking rental fee."

"Perfectly true."

"These men on our home front are dying just as combat soldiers are dying. The mortality rate from accidents is, I understand, very high. Do you begin to see what I mean? Mere money is futile. I could give them plenty of that. But they already have plenty."

Miss Davis found herself dithering.

"Am I mad, or are you leading up to the fact that you are going to throw open River Rest to war workers?"

"I am. I have four guest rooms which are going to waste and I shall rent them at a nominal fee. I would prefer letting the workers stay there for nothing, but to do so would lower their self-respect and put them under the onus of an obligation."

"Good lord."

"It is a drop in the bucket with conditions being what they are, but I shall feel happier for having done it. I am glad we have run into each other. Perhaps you will advise me as to the proper column—the 'Lodgers Wanted,' I think?"

"Don't worry, Mrs. Giles," Miss Davis said softly. "I will take care of it. I and the city editor."

"Thank you. As for the fee?"

"There won't be any. Unless it's a rebate." Miss Davis looked at Carrie Giles with fresh eyes. "You haven't changed or discovered anything new, Mrs. Giles. You're still exactly what women of your upbringing have always been." She shook off sentiment and said, "I feel like a snipe, but I still want to know why you've come to this sale and what it has to do with Kent. Also why he's overseas, but only in a sense."

"Kent did rather well with some adversaries several weeks ago. He is returning on leave to take part in a bond drive that Washington is organizing. Mr. Roosevelt will decorate him."

Miss Davis was beginning to feel glutted.

"Will you go to Washington?"

"No. But I think all these confusing emotions were what brought me here today. Last year I would have sent Spenser to bid in some object for me. I am ashamed of the fact. I brought down something of my own, this little etching. Fifty years ago it was thought that I had a flair. You know the blindness of parents? Papa was certain of genius. He made one of the attic rooms into a studio. He bought me one of Payne and Sons' Albion hand presses and an absurd amount of India paper and bond paper, as well as the minor paraphernalia. All of those things, with my genius, are now smothered under a foot of dust."

Miss Davis tried more closely to inspect the calmly drinking stag. A stocky, plain-faced, middle-aged man with thinning russet hair was planted before the etching, absorbed by it. He smiled at Miss Davis and said, "It means home to me. It's beautiful."

Miss Davis smiled automatically back and supposed he had a pool or something in a woods in Maine. Certainly there was nothing stag-like about him. She turned again to Mrs. Giles and saw her flushing delicately with pleasure.

"Mrs. Giles, I think it charming."

"My dear, don't be kind. Any illusions I may have had about my work are also under the dust with the other stuff. But I wanted to give something that I valued because it was a part of me. I thought it best to be here in case—well, I would like it to have a purchaser."

The plain-faced man turned and said to Mrs. Giles, "You mustn't feel like that. It's very good. I once studied etching at the National Academy. That was quite a few years ago. I see you prefer the gliding needle."

"Yes, there seemed a sweep."

"I'll admit that it does give a greater appearance of freedom, but I've always felt there is nothing quite like the bold use of the burin."

Miss Davis (she knew her fellow artists) saw no further profit in lingering. She said good-by and breasted the crowd and was gone.

"My name is Smith. Mrs. Giles. Dugald Smith. I know your name because I couldn't help but overhear you and Miss Davis talking."

Mrs. Giles extended her hand and received a warm, rugged grip.

"It has been a great many years since I have had the pleasure of talking with a fellow etcher, Mr. Smith."

But Mr. Smith was finished, temporarily, with art.

"I hope you won't think me abrupt," he said, "but if you had been through what my nephew and I have you would understand. You are doing a very fine thing in opening your house to defense workers. I know that as soon as Miss Davis prints the fact in her paper you will be mobbed. I would like to speak for my nephew and myself right now. We're at the Collins plant. Will you take us?"

Now that she was face to face with it as a fact rather than in warm emotional theory, Mrs. Giles felt a delicate cold shock, like a swimmer's toe before plunging into breakers. For a flash the thought of disrupting her secure and comfortable privacy with the constant presence of strangers revolted her, but it was a very brief flash.

"I shall be honored, Mr. Smith. Where and when may I send Hopkins for you and your nephew, and your things?"

CHAPTER 2

Twilight had fallen and the summer air was brooding with a hint of storm as Mrs. Giles left the exhibition hall. How kind that plain and rugged Mr. Smith had been to bid the etching in for a one-hundred-dollar bond. Sunday strollers were lethargic under the sullen humidity of the gathering weather, but Mrs. Giles was still roseate within her newly established love for her fellow men, and she felt singularly akin to the passers-by as she made her way toward the victoria drawn up at the curb.

Something of this warm and intimate kinship vanished as Hopkins creakily maneuvered himself down from the raised driver's seat, and a hard-looking specimen in his best purple double-breasted said with an overlay of jeering viciousness: "So we share and share alike. The Spartan way of living, my foot!"

Kinship thinned still further as this commentary was somewhat well received. Mrs. Giles accepted Hopkins' trembling old hand and settled back formally against gray whipcord. Several people, these newcomers to the town, stopped and watched the performance in silence.

She felt that they were speculating about her in this odd, almost tangible stillness, and for a moment her thoughts reverted to Charles Dickens with his portrayal in *A Tale of Two Cities* of the Paris mobs. She felt ashamed of this immediately. They were Americans as she was an American, and in their silent criticism the right was theirs.

She wanted a word, some password with which vocally she could tell them that they and she were one. And then she knew this was stupid because it was not true. She and her victoria with Hopkins and the roached black mare were a symbol of a favored class which in its dying, through the very apathies of its rich decay, had partially helped to bring the country to this pass. Leaders were no longer leaders when they ceased mingling with their followers and just wished to be let alone.

How could she say to them: "My husband contracted a fatal illness during the Spanish War. My son died on the banks of the Meuse. His wife could not survive him. Their child, my grandson Kent, now fights over southern seas"? Mrs. Giles knew obscurely but with a depressing certitude that even such avowals would not dispel the picture offered by the victoria and Hopkins and herself.

The carriage rolled into meager traffic, and Hopkins said, "I am sorry, madam."

"Don't be. They are tasting their day. We've finished with ours."

"Yes, madam. Shall we go home?"

"Please."

Papa, Mrs. Giles thought, would have raised a perfect hell of a scene. She had adored her father thoroughly and still did, even though she had come to realize in recent years that he had been the most thorough sort of American snob and autocrat, as well as a first-rate cutthroat capitalist. She smiled faintly at what would have been his reaction to her present intention with River Rest.

The smile did not linger.

What *was* it precisely that she had got herself into with this gesture which she still felt unshakably to be right? The simple mechanics of additions to the household became alarming, now that she considered them specifically. She had already announced her intentions to the servants and knew that they thought her mad. The house was stripped to a skeleton staff. Hopkins and Ella, both of whom had been pensioned several years ago, had willingly come back to replace Spenser and his wife after the Army had taken Spenser and his wife had joined the WAC.

Old Joel had come back, too, to potter futilely around the grounds. He had brought his niece with him to help out inside. She didn't, any more than Ophelia would have. She was a pleasant girl, Leila, but not quite bright. Not dangerous, of course. Just not quite bright. All of them, except for Leila, were well over sixty and fluttered about the place like cobwebby wraiths.

Thunder came faint across the distant hills. Mrs. Giles decided that having Mr. Dugald Smith as the first lodger was a stroke of luck. She liked his solid forthrightness, and it would be pleasant, during evenings, to continue their discussion about etching. Possibly (why not?) they might even attempt a plate or two. It seemed almost wasteful not to with all of the paraphernalia still being up in the attic studio. And she felt certain that Mr. Smith's nephew, Fergus Wade, would be equally agreeable.

But who else?

What of the others who would come to her door and be taken in? She would have her suite and Kent's room: ready for him when he came to see her after Washington. And Kent would know what it was all about. Much more clearly than Papa ever could have.

Possibly it was the depressive air, but suddenly Mrs. Giles felt terribly old and a wave of loneliness swept over her and the longing that Kent when he came would stay, that some miracle would make it possible for him never to leave her. This, she decided, was unspeakably selfish (as well as being quite impossible), and the wave receded. But it left her bleak. And, for no sound reason on earth, somewhat afraid.

The black mare turned between opened wrought-iron gates and went along a graveled driveway edged by disreputably unkempt lawns. Papa would have a fit, Mrs. Giles decided, if he could see the place now. It was odd how increasingly during her later years it was her father of whom she usually thought, rather than of her husband or of her son: of the small comforting things about childhood.

The house loomed impressively in the storm-light among great elm trees, and it felt good to be getting back home to it from the town. She paused for a moment beside the victoria, stood there with Hopkins after he had helped her out, drawing the past from him and feeling bulwarked by his familiar presence. She thought of him as a link with those whom she had loved: all of those dear lifelong friends whom she had outlived.

"I shall have to ask you to drive to town again after dinner, Hopkins."

"Yes, madam."

"Take the brougham, as it may storm. If you will go to the end of Joroloman Street you will find some tar-paper shacks. A Mr. Dugald Smith and a Mr. Fergus Wade will be waiting for you in the first shack on the right. Bring them and their luggage back here, please."

"Yes, madam."

"Thank you, Hopkins."

"I can't help saying it, but I hope nothing comes of this. Nothing bad, I mean."

"We have finished with discussions about the matter, Hopkins."

Mrs. Giles walked up shallow granite steps and into a vestibule the walls of which had been studded (by Papa) with shells that had been gathered from the seven seas. She pressed the doorbell and, while waiting, was wearied by the broad stretch of waving hay that had once been a lawn, and the storm-vivid view of the flowing river with its tree-lined banks and the further distant hills.

Thunder jarred. A bird flashed vividly on slanting wings. It made her think of Kent. It made her wish for him. To have him there.

CHAPTER 3

During the interminable time it was taking Ella to make a wraithlike journey to the door Mrs. Giles had the opportunity to wonder briefly at the sight of a pair of bicycle handle bars just visible in the once-formal shrubbery that flanked the porch.

Her legs were jumpy from so much standing at the bond sale, and it seemed hours before Ella finally let her in and offered, instead of the usual pleasant greeting, a pair of firmly compressed lips. She was a small white-haired woman and always made Mrs. Giles think (since Ella had returned to service) of a disintegrating bee.

"A Miss Effie Ashley is calling, madam."

"Ashley? I don't believe I know her."

"No. Miss Ashley is in the drawing room."

Mrs. Giles eyed an overnight bag and a good-sized cardboard box on the floor near the door.

"Whose are those?"

"Miss Ashley's, madam."

"Did she say why she is calling?"

"It's about a room," Ella said bitterly.

"Oh. Thank you, Ella."

Mrs. Giles could feel disintegration increasing in Ella as she passed her. She crossed a large tapestry rug which Papa had picked up in Aubusson and entered a great oblong room freighted with massive furnishings of teakwood and plum-colored velvet. The walls were heavy with large canvases (also picked up by Papa) depicting a gamut from the spirited charges of Arabs on horseback to such dreamy idylls as a ragamuffin stooping for a crust of bread adrift in a well-organized gutter.

Ella had turned on but few of the lamps, and Mrs. Giles brought Effie Ashley more sharply into focus as she neared the chair on which Miss Ashley was continuing to remain seated.

No, Mrs. Giles decided, I simply can't. I won't.

Years ago Mrs. Giles had seen that delightful actress, Jeanne Eagels, portraying the role of Sadie Thompson in *Rain*, and Miss Ashley's general facade revived the memory to an alarming degree. It was perfectly true that Sadie Thompson had, just prior to the final curtain, exposed a heart of gold, but it had been buried for three solid acts, and Mrs. Giles had no intention whatever of having any such acts gone through in her house.

Not with Kent coming home from Washington for part of his leave. Even without that. Not in any case.

"Miss Ashley?"

"I am. Are you Mrs. Giles?"

"Yes."

It being impossible to ask Miss Ashley either to sit down or not, Mrs. Giles yielded to her jumpy legs and took a chair herself. A waft of strong, heady scent beat against her and evoked those deplorable advertisements in which swooning women were seen in a state of total collapse (moral) as the result of a drop and a dab behind each ear.

"I'm here about a room."

"So my maid told me, Miss Ashley. I don't quite understand how you knew. The newspapers do not carry my advertisement until the morning."

"I heard you talk to that man at the bond sale, the one who bought your etching. I got your address from an old buzzard with a gardenia in his lapel who was auctioning off the stuff."

"That would be Mr. Cyrus Hastings, Sr.," Mrs. Giles said frigidly.

"So? I'm a gun inspector at the Merle plant and I've been sleeping on a cot stuffed with shredded cement in a fourth-rate flophouse. I beat it out here because I figured it would be quiet." Miss Ashley peered through heavily mascaraed eyelashes into vault-like shadows. "And God knows it is."

Mrs. Giles was rapidly being reduced into a chilled blancmange.

"I am sure, Miss Ashley, you will be able to find some other place where the atmosphere will be more compatible."

"Not a chance. Honestly, do you think I'd be here if I could have? I've pedaled around this town after leaving the shop until my legs are dead."

The voice struck Mrs. Giles as being oddly like Dawn Davis': husky and low, but not quite so pleasant. Sinister? In the way that a jungle sound would be sinister? No, it was something more difficult to define. Unbred, she thought, and then flushed slowly. What right, what earthly right in these troublous days, had a useless old woman such as herself to feel like that?

She visioned Miss Ashley in action: overalls, a grease-grimed face, dead-tired on her feet, the clashing roar of vast machines and the blinding flare of molten metal (this extraordinary vision of factory life was the result of a motion picture in which Mrs. Giles had observed one of the more hairy-chested of the male stars defeat the efforts of a foreign saboteur to blow the place up), and then, after all this, she saw Miss Ashley cycling home with dead legs to a flophouse and seeking repose on a hard, lumpy mattress. For America.

Capitulation was impulsive and swift.

"Your things are out in the hall, Miss Ashley?"

"Some of them, yes. All I could carry in one load on my bicycle."

"Hopkins will take them up. Come with me. I will show you to your room."

"How much?"

"I beg your pardon?"

"What's the price?"

"Oh—that. What would you care to pay?"

"Look, I don't know what the gag is, but they've been soaking me three and a half a night for that rejected foxhole I'm in now."

Mrs. Giles's impression of flophouses was also cinematic, and outrage filled her.

"Inconceivable!"

"I really wouldn't mind staying here. I'll feel that I'm on the wrong side of a tomb's door, but you can get used to anything."

She can't, Mrs. Giles thought, be a day over twenty-two. Not in years. And under that bright hard coating of cheap sophistication there lurked a desperate urgency. For what? Not for the need of comfortable shelter in itself. It was something more vital than that. A fugitive quality? Could you pin it down into terms of escape? No, this also did not satisfy.

"Will five dollars be satisfactory, Miss Ashley?"

"I thought so. That's thirty-five per."

"My dear, I mean a week."

Miss Ashley's eyes were weighted with suspicion.

"I'm going to tell you something, Mrs. Giles. If Mercury wasn't in the sign of the Scorpion I'd pass this up."

"I don't understand—that's astrology, isn't it?"

"It is. And I'll take a chance." Effie Ashley stood up. She glanced at an efficient polished-steel wrist watch. "I'll bicycle in and get supper and pick up the rest of my things. I will be back here at eight."

"Couldn't Hopkins get them when he drives in for Mr. Smith and his nephew? I would be most happy to have you dine this evening."

"No. I don't want board. I eat out a lot."

It was abrupt. Very abrupt, Mrs. Giles thought. Was there, she wondered as she watched the curious swiveling effect of Miss Ashley's departing rear, a touch of panic about it? She was too tired to have it matter. A nice warm bath—just soaking in it and not thinking about anything at all for a while—that would be it. Then dinner. She would feel refreshed and ready to face the arrivals later.

She headed for the stairs.

CHAPTER 4

Miss Ashley cycled with skill and swiftness. Night was fast falling, and the storm had already heralded its closeness with a few spatters of rain. She hated to get wet. Other things she didn't mind—plenty of other things—but there was something about rain-drenched clothes which drove her into a rage.

She dismounted before a paint-peeled two-story frame house with a short front lawn of sun-baked grass. This lawn was enlivened by two weedy beds of starved pansies and a large tree trunk in the hollow of which nested nasturtiums and a broken quart beer bottle.

She went inside and looked through a small pile of mail lying on an aggressively cherry table. There was nothing for her. Miss Ashley had not seriously expected that there would be, but it was better to make sure. She stood for a moment in the hall's gloom and over-lived-in smell. Just what about mail. It would never do to have it forwarded to River Rest (boy, what a joint!), certainly not the type of stationery she received.

She carried the problem upstairs with her and into a large closet which boasted one window, an iron cot, a chair, and little else. She started to fill a big zipper bag with the things still hanging on a row of hooks that were screwed lackadaisically into one wall.

"Surely you're not leaving us, dear," said the wheezy voice of Mrs. Aldershot.

Mrs. Aldershot, the woman who owned the house, had heaved her considerable girth just inside the door. She looked like something that had been cooked in oil, Italian style.

"I am."

Mrs. Aldershot indulged in a complacent sigh. Let her go. What earthly difference did it make? There were myriad others to take her place.

"Well, that's the way it is nowadays. They come and go. I often say to Mr. Aldershot, 'Will we ever settle down again and have the house to ourselves?'"

"You're doing all right."

"It's the privacy I miss. By the way, dear—or no, let me see—"

"I've settled with you up to tonight."

"Yes, now I remember that you have."

Mrs. Aldershot eyed a slinky carmine velvet dinner dress being shoved into the zipper bag. She conquered envy with the mental comment that if *that* dress could talk!

She said, "Leaving town, dear?"

Miss Ashley felt a swift surge of relief. Of course that was the answer: have the indicative stationery redirected to some point outside of Bridgehaven. Any point.

"Yes, I'm leaving town."

"Better job, perhaps?"

"Yes."

"Where will I forward your mail, dear?"

How far was far enough?

"Buffalo."

"Any address?"

"No, just Buffalo. General Delivery."

"Well, now. Too bad it isn't Detroit. Mr. Aldershot has an aunt in Detroit. She is sacrificing her rooms just as we are. Maybe she could have taken you in."

"I'm sure she could have," Miss Ashley said briefly.

Mrs. Aldershot compressed her moist little lips.

"I'll take the key now, please."

"Here it is. Good-by, Mrs. Aldershot."

"Good-by, Miss Ashley. Just Buffalo, General Delivery. I'll remember."

Mrs. Aldershot almost closed the door. From a window of her ground-floor front she had observed Miss Ashley's arrival at the house. She had been using her bicycle. The bicycle was standing right now out in the yard. Mrs. Aldershot could picture Miss Ashley in any number of odd antics but scarcely astride a wheel and pedaling her way to Buffalo. She opened the door again.

"About your bicycle, dear?"

"What about it?"

"Surely you're not just going to leave it at the station?" Miss Ashley did an excellent job of repressing a nervous start.

"I've sold it to one of the workers out at the plant. She's meeting me at the station and will take it there."

Mrs. Aldershot's smile all but vocally said maybe. However, it was none of her business, beyond her insatiable curiosity concerning other people's business. This time she closed the door.

Miss Ashley put on a serviceable raincoat. The bicycle slip had momentarily shaken her. She determined in the future to take infinite care with details, especially when in the company of the world's Mrs. Aldershots. Mrs. Giles out at River Rest would be different. Blankets of wool could be pulled over Mrs. Giles's eyes without her knowing it.

But there would be the others.

Miss Ashley went downstairs and out into the night. The rain was still only desultory, and the protecting raincoat she had put on made her not mind it.

She strapped the zipper bag onto the bicycle's luggage rack. She mounted and rode two blocks to a corner drugstore. She went inside and sat down at the soda counter.

"What will it be tonight, Miss Ashley?" an elderly wraith with wispy gray hair asked her.

"Number-two special with coffee, Jim."

How about Jim? she wondered. Was he, like Mrs. Aldershot, one of the molehills which might become a mountain? Better spike him too.

Jim put the plate of chunky macaroni, potato salad, and two slices of tongue on the counter before her. He brought coffee, butter, and rolls.

"I won't be seeing you again," Miss Ashley said.

"No? Well, now, that's too bad."

"I'm shifting to Buffalo."

He seemed politely indifferent. He said, "Nice town, Buffalo," and moved on to another customer.

Miss Ashley ate. Her appetite was excellent. She finished her coffee and looked at her watch. Yes, the call ought to get through now.

She saw that the telephone booth at the end of the store was empty. She changed three dollars into silver at the cashier's cage.

She went to the telephone booth.

She was careful about closing its door.

CHAPTER 5

The bath did not help much. Effie Ashley was with Mrs. Giles (mentally) during all of it, and regret increased that she had been swayed so swiftly into taking Miss Ashley in. There was a feeling (perhaps because desire impelled it so) that Kent was *near*. Or, if not near, that he would be with her soon.

What of Miss Ashley then? It was all right to say that Kent was a grown man, although Mrs. Giles from the telescopic viewpoint of her seventies viewed him as a large-sized child, and it was ludicrous to think of him as a tethered goat: a bait for a tigress to stalk during the few brief days he would be at River Rest, but Mrs. Giles was uncomfortable about it just the same.

When her thoughts had originally turned to taking in war workers they had not encompassed her own sex. A blind spot acquired through decades of distaste at the thought of woman labor persistently remained. No, the vacant guest rooms were to have been filled with sturdy, honest sons of toil. Definitely male. Like that good, honest, sturdy Mr. Smith. And not with any prototypes of Sadie Thompson.

Mrs. Giles's awareness of sex in toto was not far removed from the cozy corner, an architectural bedizenment which in its long-last day had surely, when you came right down to it, been designed to arouse the beast.

She selected a violet crepe from her wardrobe, and further tremors of apprehension beset her as she put it on. The nation was at war and Kent was a soldier. Mrs. Giles boiled the unpleasant picture to its essence. The result, even without cozy corners, left Kent with a headful of military information which would surely be of priceless value to the enemy, and it easily translated Miss Ashley from a Sadie Thompson into something infinitely worse: a very potent Mata Hari.

The more Mrs. Giles pondered, the more it made perfectly good sense. Miss Ashley self-confessedly had overheard her conversation at the bond sale with Mr. Smith and, presumably, its prologue with Dawn Davis. She would know that Kent was expected at River Rest on leave and would rush, as she had rushed, to install herself (plus every nefarious purpose) at River Rest too.

Spies were everywhere. A thousand posters daily told one so. And if ever Mrs. Giles had seen a spy—Sadie Thompson was now definitely out—Miss Ashley was it.

She finished hooking the violet crepe and for a pleasantly inconsequential moment thought of those nice days in the then untroubled Paris where she had bought it.

A pier glass satisfied her that her choice was right: the dress was anything but formal and still offered a touch of quiet elegance for Kent's sake should her strong intuition hit the jack pot and he should, this evening, surprise her and appear.

The pier glass also told her that she was not alone.

Leila, old Joel's niece, had made one of her typically secretive entrances into the room. Leila was willowy as Mrs. Giles was willowy, but in a much looser way. There was a flutter in it and that curious restlessness of hands, as if flowers were soon to be strewn.

Mrs. Giles repressed the start which these materializations of Leila always gave her. She liked old Joel and was grateful to him for having so willingly returned from his pensioned state of comfort even if only to potter. In consequence she felt in duty bound to like his niece, and Leila did help out about the house, no matter how witlessly or with what an innate incapability of dusting a room without giving the impression that she was conducting a séance. All of these things, with an additional touch of mild kleptomania, were a trial, but the girl was a pretty and a fundamentally harmless little thing, so Mrs. Giles put up with her quirks.

"What is it, Leila?"

One pale hand fluttered from behind Leila's back.

"It's a telegram, ma'am."

Kent—surely Kent...

"Thank you, Leila."

Leila's best Ophelia smile was shrewdly bewitching.

"If I give it to you will you tell me what's in it?"

"Yes, dear."

Mrs. Giles read the telegram.

"Mr. Kent expects to be with us for breakfast," she said.

Tears filled her eyes and she felt terribly shaken. In a fashion she was glad that Kent wasn't arriving until morning, when his return to River Rest would be a normal one with Mr. Smith and his nephew and the menacing Miss Ashley all out of the house and busied in their factories for the whole heavenly day.

She went down to dinner with a thankful and happy heart.

Leila served, offering a stuffed baked pickerel bedded on fresh garden peas, in her mood of the Delphian sibyl just brinking on profound utterances.

"Ella is having a fit," Leila said.

Mrs. Giles stopped thinking about the boniness of pickerel and their somewhat mushy texture when compared with the zing and firmness of a salt-water fish.

"What is the trouble, Leila?"

"It's that Miss Ashley."

"Well?"

"Ella took her upstairs to her room when she left her box and bag. Ella stepped into that nook by the linen room and waited."

"I must speak to Ella."

"I wouldn't. It's a very good thing she did. Forewarned, I say, is forearmed."

"Just what are you talking about, Leila?"

"I'm telling you what Ella saw from the nook. She saw Miss Ashley come out and open every door on the floor and look inside, including yours."

"How odd."

"You'll say it's odd all right when you hear what she said to Ella. Ella asked her if she was looking for something, and she told Ella she was wondering just which room had the view of the cemetery."

Leila, on this note, again offered the pickerel and garden peas. Mrs. Giles declined. Her appetite, her happiness at Kent's wire, both fled. Her most sable suspicions concerning Miss Ashley surely were confirmed. She was completely familiar with the proper literary term: Miss Ashley had been casing the house in preparation for her villainous campaign.

CHAPTER 6

Mr. Dugald Smith had not tarried at the bond sale.

He left it shortly on the heels of Mrs. Giles. He held the etching of the water-sipping stag carefully beneath one arm. Never, he considered, had the cost of a hundred-dollar bond been better spent. It was Mrs. Giles, far more than her artistic handicraft, who entranced him. He thought her a sketch and, of course, a complete push-over. How kind the gods were! At last to smile.

He hailed a taxicab and was driven to the end of Joroloman Street, from where he stepped out upon an unpaved quagmire leading to the first of a series of wretched shacks. The door of this nightmare opened into a boxlike room which was lighted by a hanging oil lantern.

He observed the figure of Fergus Wade sprawled on one of the room's two cots.

As always, whenever he looked freshly at Fergus after an absence, the artist in Smith was momentarily enchanted. No youngster outside of the classic models of early Greece had the right to be so handsome or to have a physique so well shaped. Everything was right about the fellow, including the candor that seemed to lie in Fergus' eyes, which were of a smoky blue and fringed with dark lashes.

There was only one thing about Fergus that gave Smith an occasional chilled tremor. He didn't care much about looking at Fergus' hands. They were strong hands, remarkably strong, and perfectly modeled, but Smith had seen them in action.

"The most astonishing luck," Smith said.

He placed the etching on the room's one table while Fergus stretched fluid limbs lazily on the cot, and lamplight caught the peach-down quality of his cheek.

"What's that you got?" Fergus asked with tepid curiosity.

"An etching. A pleasantly minor atrocity involving a thirsty stag. I bought it at the bond sale."

Fergus yawned again.

"Why?"

"For a sesame."

"A what?"

"That is a name with which to open doors."

Faint curiosity stirred in Fergus and then died. He held the greatest admiration for Smith, possibly for the very reason that he couldn't understand him. This in no way irritated Fergus, for few things outside of the most elemental ever did. Muscles moved in slow quicksilver as he settled on one shoulder.

"I'm hungry."

Smith drew a camp chair close to Fergus and sat down. His attitude was a good deal like that of a patient schoolteacher about to expound the simplest problem to a backward child.

"Later. This is important. We are moving to a house called River Rest right after dinner. It belongs to a Mrs. Giles. She is socially prominent and rich."

"What's she renting rooms for?"

"She has just been seized with a sharp attack of acute patriotism. She has a grandson in the Army."

"A nut."

"No, she is completely sane. Mrs. Giles and I have discovered a mutual interest in etching."

This was something that Fergus could understand. His smile was swift. It was a shy smile, appealing and very young, but Smith averted his eyes from it. It, too, although in a lesser degree than Fergus' hands, was something Smith couldn't stomach.

Pathologically the smile would have fascinated him if only from the standpoint of a scientific observer studying an impersonal specimen. Living with Fergus brought it too close. Smith knew the change that at fortunately rare intervals could come over it. It was a slight change, merely a faint distortion, but it would alter the smile's charm into a grimace which inspired both revulsion and horror.

"Are you being funny?" Fergus asked.

"I am not."

"Then what's the idea?"

"That etching on the table is the work of Mrs. Giles. It is an India proof pulled from her own press in her own studio which is in the attic of River Rest. I lingered by the etching at the exhibition on purpose, in the hope that its perpetrator would be magnetized toward it. I tell you that a setup so perfect might not happen again in a hundred years."

"I'll say it wouldn't."

"Remember this. You are to be my nephew, the son of my late sister."

"You had no sister."

Smith sighed.

"Nor, thank God, a nephew. It is the story we are to tell Mrs. Giles. We will call this sister of mine Alice. She and your father died, let us say, four years ago when their launch exploded on Long Island Sound."

"While fishing?"

"This I must beg of you. Do not embroider. Permit a simple state-ment to rest in its simplicity. If Mrs. Giles should become intrigued into wanting further details I shall be by your side and will supply them. Dur-ing dinner I will consider your background more accurately. Plain and worthy middle class. The backbone of America. Yes, something along those lines."

Fergus slid muscular legs over the edge of the cot while a soft and unhealthy light crept into his eyes.

"Will I have to do *it*, Dugald?"

A cold wind struck Smith swiftly and brought on a shiver in the close, warm room. Where there was no wind. It was the question which he had dreaded, one which he always dreaded. But in this feral world in which he lived and exercised his special talents it was a problem which, no matter how distasteful, you could not always evade. There were situ-ations in which the thing had to be done.

He hoped in this instance that such would not be the case. He had felt a genuine liking for Mrs. Giles. Not that that would ever stand in the way. The stupidity of the tenderer emotions never had.

"I think not," he said. "I think everything will run perfectly straight."

CHAPTER 7

Mrs. Giles, after a raspberry sherbet with angel food, left the table and went into the drawing room, prepared to receive.

At a quarter to eight she heard the hoofbeats of the roached black mare on the driveway, and Leila (still Delphic) shortly announced Mr. Dugald Smith and Mr. Fergus Wade.

"Ask Hopkins to take their luggage up to their rooms, Leila."

Leila agreed to do this and then as she turned to leave announced confidentially: "He's like a god."

Mrs. Giles was considerably confused by this crypticism until Smith presented Fergus. Then it did, to a fashion, make sense. She caught Leila's point and swiftly hoped there would be none of that sort of trouble there. Mild manias including the klepto were bad enough without it.

She herself felt agreeably stirred by Fergus, although certainly to no devotional extent, and was pleased with his youthful vigor and his shy, pleasant smile. She accepted his hand and thought his grip the cool, firm, line one, just right for his sturdy class of young American manhood.

"I feel pleasure in welcoming your uncle to River Rest, Mr. Wade. I have an equal one in welcoming you."

"Glad to be here," Fergus said. His altar-boy eyes looked candidly at her. "The house is nice, and you're nice too."

"Stunning!" Smith murmured as he inspected, with glazed eyes, the ragamuffin canvas with its guttered bread. "Surely a Bouguereau—or after him?"

Mrs. Giles and Fergus joined him.

"Papa said it was, Mr. Smith. A dealer whom he struck up an acquaintanceship with in the Academia di Belle Art in Venice advised him to buy it. The dealer told Papa it came from the Palazzo Pisani collection." She eyed Leila coming in with a tray. "I thought perhaps a glass of Madeira and a biscuit before you went up to your rooms?"

They sat. They were outfitted with Madeira and biscuits, and Mrs. Giles was embarked on a harmless if thoroughly pointless anecdote of how Papa had himself selected the wine while visiting the Madeira Islands, when she realized that Leila was lingering. The girl was in a state of suspended animation near the doorway, and Mrs. Giles followed the direction of Leila's gaze and brought up short against the face of Fergus.

She said sharply, "That will be all, Leila."

Fergus, at reflective length, watched Leila go.

"The port of Funchal in Madeira," he said, "isn't bad. Not hot, of course. Just isn't bad."

"You have visited there, Mr. Wade?"

"We put in there once on the way to West Africa. I was on a Barber boat. Mess boy. Spent a night at the Golden Gate Hotel on the Avenue Goncalve Zarco. Your papa may remember it."

"Papa is dead, Mr. Wade."

"Well, I'm sorry to hear it. Anyhow, I took a two-bit bus ride to the Mount and also knocked out a pair of touts who wanted to show me the sights. I knocked them out because—"

"My nephew," Smith interrupted smoothly, "sailed the seas for adventure. Ah, the eternal quest of youth! This was during that blessed period when we had finished with one war and the world was not as yet embarked on another. Fergus is heartbroken that the Navy will not accept his services. An operation. So he is doing his bit in defense work instead."

An odd look came into Smith's eyes, and an odder one into Fergus'. Oh dear! Mrs. Giles thought. I *must* somehow get rid of her. This is going to be much more difficult even than I imagined. She observed Effie Ashley's sultry approach down the long living room. "Sinuous" alone was the word for it.

Miss Ashley came to a draped rest and summed up with a leisured inspection the several assets of Smith and Fergus.

"I want a key, Mrs. Giles," she said. "I don't care whether it's for the front door or not, but I want to be able to go out and then get back in here again without pushing a bell. That fugitive from a midsummer night's dream who let me in gives me the delirium with tremors."

"I shall see that you have a key, Miss Ashley."

"Thanks."

"A fellow lodger?" Smith asked.

A lifetime of habit made Mrs. Giles's introductions complete and formal, and the very act of going through with this familiar ritual restored the moment to a semblance of social balance.

"I see you wasted no more time than my nephew and I did in seeking this haven, Miss Ashley. It smacks of divine guidance, or is there a Sunday evening paper in town I've missed?"

"I heard you fixing things up with Mrs. Giles at the bond sale. It sounded good." Miss Ashley glanced with undisturbed openness at Fergus. "It's looking a good deal better too."

Mrs. Giles was not entirely displeased with the boldness of this optical attack. For Kent's sake and, to a lesser degree, for Leila's, although she felt confident of being able to manage *that*. But was this fair? Not really. Even though young Mr. Wade was a stranger and obviously quite competent in taking care of himself, were not the production secrets of his factory as valuable to the enemy as were the military ones of Kent? Almost? But in any case wouldn't Miss Ashley put Mr. Wade on ice until she had first drained Kent?

Her head was beginning to swim, and Mrs. Giles was grateful when Mr. Smith said that he and his nephew would retire and enjoy the first good night's sleep they would have had since they had come to Bridgehaven.

"I will ask Ella to show you which your rooms are," Mrs. Giles said. "And you, Miss Ashley? Will you be retiring too?"

Miss Ashley permitted amazement to settle on her face.

She said, "At half-past eight?"

CHAPTER 8

Mrs. Giles carried unease upstairs with her.

She took off the violet crepe and slipped on a wrapper, then went into her living room. No air came in through its open windows. She stood at one for a while looking out across the driveway off to the river. The summer shower had petered out, and a full moon patterned violet high lights on the shrubbery and grass.

Through the front windows of the drawing room just below came a scratching screech, then a full-toned blast of Johann Strauss's "Wiener Blut" waltz. The volume decreased, and Mrs. Giles felt a surge of outraged anger that that woman had *dared*—but why not? It was in character, and character was something which so rarely could be changed. Having taken her in, why should she draw the line at Miss Ashley using the victrola? Certainly a guest could have. But even so Mrs. Giles remained shaken.

"Wiener Blut" was cut short in the middle. A heavenly arrangement of "Künsterleben" didn't even get to the middle. "Voices of Spring" lived for six bars. Silence.

Mrs. Giles sighed deeply and selected a book on the downfall of the Roman Empire with the hope that it would make her sleepy enough to take her mind off things. It didn't. The only historical work which had ever jounced her had dealt with Napoleon, and Mrs. Giles had been horrified on discovering that Napoleon wasn't all he was cracked up to be.

She read with admirable determination for two hours, until the clock struck eleven, but persistently in her thoughts was an awareness of how subtly and yet how decisively the basic atmosphere of her house had changed.

It felt no longer *like* her house.

In its silence, in their several rooms, were the three strangers, and all of them had keys. There were plenty of keys, for the family had been large and Papa had been completely broad-minded about letting every member have one, his theory being that locks were no bars to any sprouting of wild oats: his own sowings presumably having taught him this.

The impressionable stillness was disturbing, more so even than had been Miss Ashley's quickly disgusted rendezvous with the recordings.

It was a blessing she hadn't come upon Kent's private stock. Mrs. Giles could stand them when Kent played them, because anything that Kent did was all right, but she was sure that if Miss Ashley had done so—especially that one with the hot licks—her nerves would have snapped.

What, now, were the strangers about? Conjectures obsessed her. Mr. Smith she felt sure of. Bed and sleep would have claimed him. But of his sturdy handsome nephew and that seductive *agent*—a myriad of distressing surmises flitted through the heavy night air with the persistency of gnats.

Tell me (Mrs. Giles could almost hear Miss Ashley's husky voice drifted at Fergus through clouds of that reeking perfume), how many gyroscopes came off the assembly line last week? Or some such pertinent question cunningly framed for the later delight and comfort of the Axis.

She shut the book, its secondary worthiness as a soporific having failed. She turned the lights out in the living room and in the bedroom and went to bed. Curious how that sensing, that *feeling* of Kent's nearness persisted. He couldn't be close, of course. The wire had been sent from Washington.

What was he like now? Would the terrible hours and months of active combat have changed him? Stamped his brash, fine youth with some imprint of bestial iron? She thought not. She prayed not. His rare letters had been increasingly unintelligible in part, with a confusing new vocabulary that housed such indigestible pearls as knuckleheads, gizmos, pogie bait, boon dockers, and gloms.

A terrible suspicion seized Mrs. Giles that Miss Ashley, instead of being bewildered, would know exactly what Kent meant. Surely such linguistics must enter in the curriculum of Gestapo schools.

Scuffle?

Mrs. Giles held her breath. A scuffle was what it had sounded like: outside on the graveled driveway. She got out of bed and put on her wrapper and slippers. She did not turn on a light but hurried to a window and looked down. She could see nothing and the night was quiet again, but she went into the living room to try the view from there.

Clearly it struck her, clear in the moonlight, like ice in swift congealment around her heart: Kent's rangy, beloved figure standing down there on the driveway, and with him, with her face turned up to him and the moonlight exposing the—yes, the passionate earnestness of her expression—was Miss Ashley.

Mrs. Giles closed her eyes and gripped the back of a chair for support. Rage filled her more than fear as the scuffle sound recurred to her. The most elementary sort of common sense tried to reassure her that the tableau with its implications of intimacy was too coincidental (and far too sudden) to be possible, even for the seductive machinations of a Miss Ashley. They *couldn't* have known one another (optical testimony shouted that they did) previously… Mrs. Giles took another look.

It was worse. Miss Ashley's face was still turned up toward Kent's, and her voice, although whispering, was able from its very intensity to reach Mrs. Giles's ears.

"*We must. I insist!*"

Mrs. Giles no longer waited. At no matter what cost to Kent's opinion of her it was time for the personal touch. She felt her way through darkness along the familiar hall and started downstairs. Halfway there was a turning accented by an ornate post on which stood a statue in bronze of winged Mercury poised on one tiptoe for flight. Mrs. Giles waited until the smacking sound of it hitting the hall floor subsided.

She went on down. She opened the front door and went through the vestibule onto the porch. A strong effort helped to make her voice sound warmly welcoming: "Kent darling—I heard your voice."

Her own voice died as the moonlight betrayed an empty driveway. Silence and emptiness were where Kent and Miss Ashley had been. Had the sound of the falling statue sent them into flight? *Why* flight? Why should Kent, from his own home…? Gravel was sharp through the thin soles of her slippers as she stepped down onto the drive. She walked as far as the branch curve to the stables. No one. Nothing moved in the whole silent night.

Mrs. Giles started back for the house, skirting because of the sharp gravel the grassy edge of the driveway that fringed the evergreens and shrubs. She caught at a coster blue spruce to save herself from falling and then looked down to see what she had stumbled over.

A man's leg.

It was not Kent. The cloth was of dark tweed, and Kent had been in uniform. The shoe was black, and even in the soft moonlight it had an air of fine leather and good bench workmanship. Like the shoes which Papa had always worn.

Shock lost its initial protective numbness, and Mrs. Giles began to tremble. She choked back a scream. She conquered an urge to run for the shelter of the house. She had to know. For Kent's sake she had to know. Then maybe she would be able to decide what must be done.

She parted the azaleas among which the man had fallen. The face was a distinguished one, elderly, around sixty, Mrs. Giles imagined. Looking down at it, she thought of ambassadors and foreign courts. It was no one whom she knew or had ever known. The eyes were wide open. Too open. Sightless, dead.

The man's coat was thrown (jerked, it looked like) open, and she could see the handle of the knife now, its blade being sunk through the white dark-stained shirt. A wave of nausea almost caused her to fall forward, but she steadied herself. Dimly in memory returned the sound of the scuffle which she had heard and this time with its new significance of a man stabbed to his death.

No hurry now. Mrs. Giles drew a breath in deeply to conquer giddiness, then her eyes were held by a spot of silver, bright in the moonlight, which lay touching the fingers of the man's right hand. It struck her, oddly, as being something with which she was familiar, and she stooped and picked it up.

She knew.

She felt she must have known instantly what they would be: the platinum bracelet and Army identification tag which she had had made and had given to Kent when he had entered the service. The moonlight was strong enough to identify the numbers and the lettering and to crush Mrs. Giles with the wrenching assurance that this was so.

But it did not crush her. All her knowledge of him, from the days when he had been a baby until war had taken him away, fully assured her that Kent had not done this thing. Until war—no. Not even this appearance in the night when he had wired he would not be here until morning, neither that clandestine touch nor the utterly inexplicable scene with Miss Ashley…

Miss Ashley. It was Miss Ashley who had enmeshed him in this murderous act. Miss Ashley was the murderess, her undoubtedly well-practiced hand the wielder of the knife. By what witch's sorcery had she first evoked and then cast her spell on Kent? What powers, what dark devices had she employed to bring him to the spot at the moment when the deed was done?

What of the police? Mrs. Giles's reaction was at once to obey all precepts of the law and summon them. And then? She saw herself telling them: "I heard a scuffle on the driveway. From my living-room window I saw my grandson and Miss Ashley talking. I found that stranger stabbed to death. Beside his hand I found my grandson's Army identification tag."

No.

She saw the end of many things for Kent: his value to Washington's bond drive shattered, a hero besmirched, Mr. Roosevelt with the medal and no breast to pin it on, while Kent for dreary days, perhaps months, was confined in a federal prison awaiting court-martial for the murder of a civilian.

Her sense insisted that on the other hand Kent might have some perfectly rational explanation which would clear him from any involvement at all. But if this were so, why his clandestine appearance and present flight? Had Miss Ashley during that brief and inexplicable moment so strongly meshed him in her power?

Had it been Kent? Uniforms could make men look extraordinarily alike, certainly so in moonlight and from the angled view that she had had from the upstairs window. Kent's identification tag spiked that. No plot so lurid, so involved as to include the tag being stolen from Kent in Washington and then whisked by magic here to be dropped beside the hand of a corpse, could obtain even during such mischievous days as these.

Somewhere the answer lay to this problem of what to do. Not with Kent, but with Miss Ashley. Perhaps among her things? Mrs. Giles, who normally would have recoiled at the thought of rifling a guest's personal belongings, was far past any recoiling. And now would be the moment to do it, while Miss Ashley (definitely astride her broomstick) was abroad in the night.

Azaleas again concealed the dead man. All but the leg. Delay seemed of the essence to Mrs. Giles now that her course was charted to by-pass the police. She stooped and shoved, and then the leg was concealed too. An ague of fever gripped her, but she shook it off and started for the house with Kent's bracelet and identification tag clenched in her hand.

She fumbled in the darkness until she found the bronze statue of Mercury, then carried it up and set it back on the landing post. She went to her rooms and shoved the bracelet and identification tag deep under lingerie in a dresser drawer. Then she hastened down the hallway to Miss Ashley's door.

She rapped.

She turned the handle and stepped in. A lamp flashed on brilliantly, and Miss Ashley, alarmed under bedcovers, said sharply: "What is it?"

Blood slowly flushed into Mrs. Giles's face. The dread importance of murder curiously became insignificant for the moment before this surge of mortified embarrassment. Mrs. Giles accomplished a swift marshaling of her wits.

"I heard a sound of something falling out in the hallway, Miss Ashley. It worried me, and after a while I thought I had better just come in and see whether you were all right."

Miss Ashley's face continued expressionless. So did her voice.

"I heard it too. It woke me up. A single thump seemed mild for a house like this. I've been expecting clanking chains. Thanks anyhow for coming. And now, good night."

"Good night, Miss Ashley."

Miss Ashley waited until Mrs. Giles's fingers touched the doorknob.

"Better change your slippers," she said, "or you'll catch cold. Those are wet."

CHAPTER 9

Mrs. Giles retraced her steps along the silent hallway to her rooms. Inside them, reaction set in.

She turned on lamps and poured a small glass of sherry from a bottle which she kept in the medicine cabinet on the bathroom wall. She felt distressingly faint. She returned to the living room and sank into an arm-chair beside an open window. She sipped sherry, growing almost immediately somewhat warmer and better for it.

How much time had elapsed between the moment when she had last glimpsed Kent and Miss Ashley down on the driveway and when she had re-entered the house? Mrs. Giles thought it would have been twenty minutes fully.

Twenty minutes during which such an accomplished graduate at skullduggery as Miss Ashley could with ease have flitted back up to bed (certainly during that moment while Mrs. Giles had stood at the branch road peering toward the stables) and thus have been prepared to greet any alarms which might transpire with sleep-drugged eyes and that nightgown which—well!

What boldness, what superb effrontery on Miss Ashley's part to have seized the bull by its horns with that parting crack about the dew-wetted slippers. With one stroke it had reduced Mrs. Giles to the disadvantage of being on the defensive.

Mrs. Giles clearly read Miss Ashley's true import wrapped up in the statement's deceitful simplicity: You were outside on the rain-wet grass. The sound of the scuffle on gravel brought you to your window. You saw me and you recognized Kent. (This was another reason, Mrs. Giles decided, why Miss Ashley had so cannily hustled up again to bed: to be awakened from sleep if Mrs. Giles came to question her.) You came downstairs and went out and discovered the body. Otherwise you would have demanded of me frankly and normally why Kent had not come in to greet you and where he had gone. You are afraid to call the police. You are afraid to accuse or even to question me because you do not know what knowledge or power I have for harming your grandson. Between you and me there must exist a truce of silence.

All that in a statement of eleven words.

And it was true. Mrs. Giles was thoroughly aware of the bonds which tied her hands. There was nothing she could do and nothing she could say until she had talked with Kent. And if he, too, should copy Miss Ashley and erect a barrier of silence, what then?

She found a small solace in the philosophy that things usually work out satisfactorily if they are *right*. Age had taught her the truth of this. Age also had taught her the dangers which lurk in any interference based on a laudable purpose of trying to be helpful. It rarely if ever was so and usually served only to roil a muddy situation still further.

Like that time years ago when Papa had tried to be helpful about her undying love for the grocer's delivery boy. Papa's well intentioned if pyrotechnical methods had only prolonged love's death struggle to an all-time high: one which had fallen just short of the final act of *Tristan und Isolde*.

Oddly, this remembrance soothed Mrs. Giles and quieted the sharper edges of her nerves. She went to bed but not at once to sleep, for in the darkness, tempered by frail moonlight, hovered the soul-sickening vision of that body under the azaleas: a frame, a lump no more significant than earth, but it had moved and breathed and had lived its days for good or evil, or the usual balanced ration of both.

Almost more than murder itself, it distressed her to dwell on the indignity of the body lying down there, and her self-reproach was rapidly approaching a point of torment when utter, absolute exhaustion took matters into its own hands and collapsed her into sleep.

Leila woke her. She carried a Bridgehaven *Gazette* in her hand.

Leila had on her important look. Oh dear, Mrs. Giles thought, she's been up to something. Then Kent, Miss Ashley, the identification tag, and the body in the azaleas stepped out from the last veil of slumber, and the bright sunny morning crashed in shreds around her.

"It's all on the front page," Leila said. "A picture of the house and you in that dress you wore to the Assembly a few years ago and all."

(*Impossible—the police would have wakened her...*)

"It says," Leila went on, "that your renting rooms to war workers should serve as a shining example to the womanhood of America and especially asks Washington papers to please copy. It also says all sorts of nice things about Mr. Kent and calls him our first local hero. Will I read it to you?"

Relief came in a partial flood.

"No, Leila. Just put it down on the table. What time is it?"

"It's half-past seven, and Mr. Hopkins telephoned the station, and Mr. Kent's train is late and won't be in until almost ten. They told him something about a derailed freight car holding up the line."

"Thank you."

The important look grew more decisive.

"Here."

Leila reached into an apron pocket and handed Mrs. Giles a five-dollar bill.

"What's this for?"

"I fixed it all by myself. He got here half an hour ago, and as he's on night shift he wanted to go right to bed. He gave me the five dollars for the rent for the week, and I told him how lucky he was as there was only one room left. He went straight up to it and told me to call him at four o'clock this afternoon."

Bleakness added itself to the chill surrounding Mrs. Giles's heart. How unimportant, how maddeningly distracting was the room-renting gesture in view of that body down below in the azaleas.

"Oh, Leila!"

Importance vanished, leaving a spanked look on Leila's sensitive face, and a trembling lip.

"Didn't I do right? I only wanted to save you bother, and you told me last night you didn't want me to wake you until half-past seven."

"Yes, clear. You were quite right. Most helpful. Who is this man?"

Leila bloomed afresh.

"He's ever so nice. His name is Mr. Jefferson Parling. He looks just like Humphrey Bogart."

Mrs. Giles shut her eyes. She was fairly familiar with Mr. Bogart's characterizations on the screen, and to have anyone of those blood-throttling roles in the house was the last straw. That was all, she told herself dismally, that was needed: a good, well-typed Menace.

Furthermore, he was on night shift and he would be sequestered within the house during daytime. Even if he were to sleep the daylight hours through and she didn't see him, she would know he was there.

"Have the others gone, Leila?"

"Yes. Mr. Smith and Mr. Wade left at seven and Miss Ashley at a quarter past. Oh dear, but he's handsome."

Mrs. Giles decided the moment was at hand for taking a bull by the horns herself.

"Leila!"

"Well?"

"I shall have to ask Joel to take you away from here if there is any of that."

"Of what?"

"You know what I mean. I refer to Mr. Wade."

Leila managed to look both secretive and crushed. Her hands fluttered in a gesture which Mrs. Giles under less pressure would have interpreted as "Perish the thought!"

"I mean it, Leila, and that will be all. Tell Ella that I will have tea and toast and will breakfast more fully with Mr. Kent after he arrives."

Leila vanished mystically, and Mrs. Giles got out of bed. She still held in her hand the five-dollar bill. It began to assume the characteristics she had attributed to its donor, and she put it on the dresser with a faint shudder and, going into the bathroom, turned water on in the tub.

Then she could hold herself from doing it no longer. She walked to a living-room window and looked down.

She could almost see, she thought, the section of the azaleas where the body lay. The general view was quietly serene: a normal summer's morning with the grasses all fresh from last evening's shower. She leaned out across the sill. She could see nothing disturbed about the shrubbery's matted tops.

A bicycle whizzed around the curve in the drive, and a burly young man shouted up at her: "Is this River Rest?"

"It is."

"Got any left?"

"Left? I beg your pardon?"

"Rooms—them things you got the ad in about. Are they all taken?"

"Yes."

"Okay, Grandma."

The wheel turned, scorched off, and Mrs. Giles withdrew from the window. She found herself shaking, although "sizzling" might have been a better word. She picked up the Bridgehaven *Gazette*, and pride filled her as she read its splendid tribute to Kent, and determination was strong to do everything in her power to shield him and the service he represented from the slightest blot.

She turned to the column devoted to herself, and blood pressure mounted as, at its close, she found herself being publicly slated for a niche in history alongside such women as Eleanor Roosevelt, Madame Chiang Kai-shek, and Betsy Ross.

She managed to bathe and put on a dress of heliotrope linen. It had a pocket in its blouse, and she went to the dresser and took out Kent's bracelet and identification tag. She folded them loosely in a handkerchief and arranged it in the pocket.

Then Mrs. Giles stood quite still.

CHAPTER 10

Leila's voice had come back to her: "Mr. Smith and Mr. Wade left at seven and Miss Ashley at a quarter past."

Miss Ashley was out of the house.

More than ever it seemed of importance to Mrs. Giles swiftly to find out what she could. She stepped out into the cool quiet hallway and walked along it past the doors to Mr. Smith's room and Mr. Wade's. She stopped before Miss Ashley's.

Directly across the hall was the door to the room which Leila had just rented to the fourth lodger. She tried to recall his name. Purl-something? Parl-something? All she could think of was Bogart. No sound came from his room. Perhaps he was already asleep. Perhaps he wasn't. Perhaps he was sitting in there and brooding with a dead-pan look and his mind a-boil with schemes of sabotage.

Mrs. Giles opened Miss Ashley's door and went inside, closing the door behind her. The room was surprisingly neat. Nothing was strewn about, as Mrs. Giles had expected things to be: a stocking here, a slipper kicked there, and that nightgown left dropped where it had been stepped out of. No, Miss Ashley's belongings were all properly in place.

This well-ordered effect surprised Mrs. Giles decisively as it seemed out of character. It also increased her repellent distaste of the job which faced her.

Ten minutes did the trick and left Mrs. Giles, so far as she could see, just where she had started. Nothing. No papers of any sort. And certainly none of the prescribed paraphernalia for Miss Ashley's Mata-Haran occupation, such as invisible inks, pertinent drugs, or small, flat black automatics which could be whipped out during moments of stress from beaded evening bags or chinchilla muffs.

Mrs. Giles grew frightened. Was not this very void of things a strong confirmation that her suspicions were sound? It was unnatural that a normal young woman (granting just for the moment that Miss Ashley was a normal one) should be away from home for a lengthy time and not have with her the slightest ties, such as letters, photographs, mementos, some bond to link her with her roots.

She had no past.

Mrs. Giles then paradoxically decided that Miss Ashley certainly did have one, but not a nice past, not one that you could put out openly on your dresser top or leave lying around in a desk drawer. It was all in Miss Ashley's head. That's where she kept it, cleverly, securely, utterly safe from prying hands or eyes. The very height of superb artifice lay in the thought.

Mrs. Giles left the room and went downstairs.

Her second and far worse task lay before her. No one was about. She opened the front door and stepped through the vestibule onto the porch, where she breathed deeply of the fine morning air, as if (*should* there be lurking eyes) to give her movements an innocent motivation.

She forced herself to step down onto the gravel drive and walk along it with casual pauses during which she hoped her gestures and expression portrayed a passing interest in the state of the shrubbery's health.

With her whole heart, as each step drew her closer, she prayed that a miracle would have occurred. Seeming ones so very frequently did happen in those exciting stories she had such a weakness for. Lots of times in the stories the Body, when you went to look at the scene of the crime again or else were leading the detective to it, would have vanished. Later, of course, it would always pop up in the most unexpected places, and in this case Mrs. Giles most fervently wished it would do just that. In as remote a one as possible.

There was no miracle.

As she parted the azalea tops Mrs. Giles saw that the body was still there. A bee buzzed importantly and a dragonfly darted eccentrically in the warm sun. A sickish sensation would have brought on a fainting spell if a voice shouting "Hi!" hadn't shocked her into an atavistic stance of defense. Mrs. Giles permitted the azalea tops to close and turned around.

Another bicycle was spraying gravel to a stop. Another burly youngster jumped from it and shook off sweat from a glistening face.

"I want one of your rooms," he gasped. "There's a field of about twenty strung out behind me. Did I make it in time?"

Mrs. Giles by now had fair control over her breath.

"I'm sorry." (Strangely enough, looking into his eager young face, she really was. How much better—what heaven, really—would it be to have a fine boy like this one under her roof rather than that wicked female spy.) "They're gone."

"All of them?"

"Yes, all."

"Well, thanks anyhow." The youngster glanced over his shoulder. "Better duck. They're jamming the gate."

Mrs. Giles cast one look toward the gateway, where a tangled mass of bicycles plus belligerently shouting riders were throwing all courtesies of the road to the winds in an effort to force a way through.

"I wonder," Mrs. Giles said with a slender smile—she would have liked to give him a real warm one, but her heart was too stricken with the knowledge of the body lying so close to them—"whether after I've ducked you would be kind enough to tell them that the rooms are filled?"

"Leave them to me."

"Thank you."

Mrs. Giles hurried into the house. Leila was hovering in the entrance hall.

"Your tea is ready."

"Thank you, Leila."

"Are you well?"

"Well?"

"Yes. You look white and sick. You look like Mamma looked just before she had her stroke."

"I'm not sick, dear. I'm perfectly all right. *Perfectly*."

CHAPTER 11

Mrs. Giles found small relief in the hot, fragrant tea.

She sipped it slowly and looked with bleak eyes at the paintings which Papa had bought for the walls of the large handsome dining room. Even as a child Mrs. Giles had thought that Papa had overdone a good thing a little in his wholehearted adherence to that distant day's trend. It was a trend which had leaned heavily, for dining rooms, toward still-life groupings of vegetables, loaves of bread, wine bottles, fish by Chase, and slices of roast beef by Chardin. Pictorial encouragements for hearty appetite.

Whom could she produce as a countercheck to Miss Ashley for Kent? To break the evil spell. So many of the girls in Kent's set had joined one or another of the women's service organizations and were stationed in distant places. So very few were left in town—the barest handful, really—and as Mrs. Giles sorted them over she admitted dispiritedly that not one possessed a tenth of the high-powered (no matter how wretched) allure or sultry good looks of Miss Ashley. They were a pallid field.

Her bemusings were shattered by Leila's coming in and announcing Dawn Davis. Not only announcing her but actually showing her in.

Miss Davis remained every bit the smart society columnist of the Bridgehaven *Gazette* in spite of the fact that eight in the morning was, for her, the middle of the night. Her attack, too, was as bold as ever.

"I'm here for a follow-up," she said, drawing a chair from the table and sitting down. "It's one of the best human-interest stories so far this year. How does it feel to be sprouting into a national heroine? I think that Betsy Ross touch was especially good, don't you?"

Mrs. Giles summoned a social smile. Here, she told herself, is the press, and how shortly might it not become advisable for Kent's sake to have it on their side!"

"Miss Davis will have tea, Leila."

"No." Miss Davis conquered a shudder. "No tea."

"Coffee? Surely something?"

"Nothing. Thank you very much. I judge from that battered mob I plowed through as it straggled away that you're already filled up?"

"Yes, the rooms are all taken. That will be all, Leila." Miss Davis, who was well in the clutches of a hang-over, did not find the state of her nerves improved as she watched Leila's phantasmal departure.

"Does she always do that?"

"Leila? Do what, Miss Davis?"

"Float. Look as though she were waving chiffon. Oh, you must know what I mean."

"Leila is a little vague. She's a dear girl, perfectly all right. Just vague."

"I'd say she was deficient in gravitation. Look, Mrs. Giles, do you mind if I interview the new roomers?"

"I'm afraid that just now it's not possible. Mr. Smith and his nephew, Mr. Wade, and Miss Ashley have all left for their work. Mr. Parling"—the name came in a flash—"is on night shift and so is sleeping."

Dawn Davis pounced.

"Miss! *Miss*? Ashley, is it? Do tell me about her."

No. Definitely no.

"I understand she is a gun inspector, and that is all I know."

"Oh, but that won't do at all. I want the human reactions, her relief at being able to find a room in a magnificent house such as this one. Her awe."

Tea all but spilled from the cup.

"Awe?"

"Certainly. Wasn't she overcome with it?"

"I found Miss Ashley quite—well, self-contained."

"Not for my column she won't be. What about the three men? Surely you see what I'm after. From-hovels-to-palaces sort of thing."

"Mr. Smith and his nephew are plain, pleasant gentlemen. Mr. Parling I have still to meet. Leila arranged his staying here before I got up. I am sorry. I'm afraid there is nothing"—Mrs. Giles gagged slightly—"dramatic about any of them. And I do hope your paper will just let the matter drop." Dawn Davis cast a fly on fresh waters.

"Now what's the latest on Kent? We want a follow-up on him too. Anything further about his arrival?"

It was so abrupt that Mrs. Giles could not repress a start. She felt herself paling.

"Kent's train is due in here from Washington around ten," she said swiftly.

"This morning?" Miss Davis all but screamed it.

"Yes. He wired last night that he would be home for breakfast."

"Why, that's in a couple of hours from now. You'll be at the station to meet him, of course?"

Chill gripped Mrs. Giles afresh as she sensed new dangers: Dawn Davis would certainly arrange to be on the platform with a press photographer prepared to snap Kent descending from the train and gathering her (Mrs. Giles) in one of his swift, exuberant embraces.

Possibly a regular news reporter would be with Miss Davis. The Bridgehaven *Gazette* might even cook up an impromptu demonstration of welcome. Mayor Saltensburg was famous for dropping everything and tearing off into the limelight whenever a camera was slated to click. The City Fathers. The City Band. All mustered within under two hours? It could be done. There was power in the press.

And Kent would not step down from that train.

Kent was already in town. Concealed somewhere, waiting since last night to show up at the house at the moment he had announced. An accomplice, no matter how innocent a one, in the murder of that ghastly, pitiful body beneath the azaleas. Kent, a helpless pawn enmeshed within this truly desperate situation through that devastating young woman's wiles.

Bright determination spread itself across Miss Davis' face. She stood up.

"I'll run along now." She cast a planning look over her shoulder from the doorway. "There isn't much time, but don't worry. We'll break out as much ticker tape as we can."

Mrs. Giles sat quite still.

Automatically she finished her cup of tea. She rang a silver bell. She said, when Leila came in, "Ask Hopkins, please, to bring the brougham around at half-past nine. I have decided to drive to the station and meet Mr. Kent."

She went upstairs to her room. A leaden hour went by.

During it Mrs. Giles had devised a tentative plan. She put on a white linen jacket and a conservative leghorn hat. She selected a pair of knitted gloves from a dresser drawer. Her face, as she saw it in the mirror, startled her.

In desperation she found and applied some rouge.

CHAPTER 12

The tumbrel rolled.

A tumbrel was what the brougham felt like right then to Mrs. Giles as the streets of Bridgehaven slid slowly past. Her plan was quite clear by now and it would work, she thought, if everything was to go all right. Kent was so odd about departures and arrivals. Not odd, really. Just frank.

Many people disliked being seen off or welcomed on a station platform, but Kent had the strength of mind to come right out and say so. He always claimed there was nothing worse than that set grin of parting and the vocal clichés which unavoidably accompanied it.

So for years Kent's good-bys and hellos had always taken place at the house. Even when he had gone away the last time to that destination which had lain in Mrs. Giles's heart so heavily as Unknown, her hand had been waved to him from the porch. It had waved until Ella had stopped her and told her that the carriage was out of sight.

So he wouldn't be expecting anyone to meet him now.

And so, Mrs. Giles had reasoned, if she were to create a diversion Kent's non-appearance from the train might be covered. It was perfectly feasible. The train was a crack flier and usually seemed endless in length. Traffic was terrifically heavy, and there were always many men in uniform on board.

Mrs. Giles's intention was to throw her lifelong habit of reticent reserve in public places overboard. Carefully she rehearsed the scene in her mind. First a good audible cry of recognition to establish the pretense of having seen Kent on the platform of the forward car of the long train. Then (the prospect chilled her) she planned to *run* along the platform, with the assurance that Miss Davis, plus all cohorts, would be drawn in her wake.

This would later leave it open for Kent to say that he had got off from the rear car and had missed them. Then, not expecting to have been met by Mrs. Giles in the first place, he could claim that he had hurried to a taxi and gone out to the house. Mrs. Giles hoped to be clever enough in her words of greeting, when she returned to River Rest and would find Kent waiting for her, to throw Kent a lead and make this explanation for him both natural and simple.

She looked at her brooch-watch. It was a quarter to ten, and the facade of Merkwin's Emporium sliding past the brougham's window on her right reassured her that the depot was but a few blocks farther away. Her fingers released the watch and then touched for an instant the outline of Kent's identification tag which still lay folded in the handkerchief in the pocket of her blouse. It, too, had a part in her plan.

She steeled herself as Hopkins swung right onto Maple Street and the Union Station loomed at the block's farther end. It had seemed to Mrs. Giles during her glimpse of it that an exceptionally large crowd was gathered on the sidewalk before the main entrance, an impression which was verified as the brougham drew up to a stop and the flushed face of Dawn Davis looked in through a lowered window.

"We've accomplished marvels," Miss Davis screamed. "We even dashed out to the broadcasting station and persuaded them to break in on *Unwanted Wife* with a news flash about Kent's arrival. They cut *just* while Felicia Halloway was being told by young Dr. Mortlake that her disease was incurable and she'd be dead before her husband and the woman he'd run off with could be located. My dear, simply at the *height* of the suds."

Mrs. Giles smiled grimly. She graciously permitted herself to be photographed while Hopkins handed her out of the brougham. She greeted Mayor Saltensburg with that touch of queenliness which she knew he expected of her. She rested finger tips on the crook of his arm and allowed him to conduct her along a police-opened lane through the station and out onto the platform. It was there all right: the City Band. And also, it seemed, most of Bridgehaven.

The din was indescribable. Voices were at full cry in the pressing crowd, and the band was blaring a march which Mrs. Giles had never heard before and sincerely hoped she would never have her eardrums split with again.

"Just as Lieutenant Giles steps down from the train," Mayor Saltensburg shouted at her, "the boys will break into 'Hail, the Conquering Hero Comes.'"

"Most thoughtful."

"My message of welcome is going to be broadcast. That's the mike they're setting up over there. Then your grandson will say a few well-chosen words. Not much. We don't want to take the edge off the reception tomorrow afternoon."

"The what?"

"Reception," Mayor Saltensburg shouted above a fortissimo passage for bassoons and cymbals. "Over at the City Hall tomorrow afternoon at five. Key to the city. Cocktails. The governor. In fact, the works. Like it?"

Mrs. Giles gibbered unintelligibly.

"I knew you would," Mayor Saltensburg screamed. "Nothing too good for that grandson of yours. The town is his, and everything that's in it."

Including (the thought stabbed Mrs. Giles while the smile remained frozen on her face) the body out at home and a dark shroud of heaven knew what dangers that enveloped him.

A whistle blew.

Thunder crescendoed and decreased and the train was in.

Mrs. Giles opened her lips to go into her act. Her planned cry of false recognition choked with shock. That was Kent. Kent, really Kent, was standing on the platform of a car that jerked to a stop right in front of her. Their eyes met, and she sent her heart out to him. Her broken sob of "Oh, my *darling*!" was drowned in a shattering crash of "Hail, the Conquering Hero Comes," done in full brass and percussion.

For a long moment their eyes held, shoving the sea of noise and people and flicking flash bulbs apart from them, creating a special privacy in the public clamor, but no message came from him, no *special* message that Mrs. Giles could interpret to relieve her misery. He looked strong and deeply tanned and hard, like a burnished copper statue almost, in the style of that Belgian sculptor who was so clever with men. Men. Perhaps that was it. For her grandson was no longer a boy.

The moment broke, and then with a rush he was holding her in his arms. "What in God's name is this?" he said in her ear.

She managed to keep her tears from flowing and to mumble something back, then the crowd exuberantly broke through the police lines and crushed her apart from Kent. She thought they were mauling him, but they weren't. Most honestly they were welcoming him, even though his uniform would probably be in shreds before they got through with it.

Shreds…might not the perfect moment be now? Mrs. Giles took the handkerchief from her blouse pocket and carefully, crumpling the bracelet and identification tag in it, dabbed at her eyes. She stiffened rigidly as a flash bulb flicked white stars in her eyes and a news photographer shouted at her: "*That's* the stuff we want, sister."

Her plan had primarily included a dropping of the identification tag somewhere along the station platform during her false-identification scene of Kent. She had had confidence that it would be assumed that Kent had lost it at the station on his arrival. This hearty, good-natured mauling the crowd was giving him, this miracle of his actually having come on the train made the setup seem perfect to Mrs. Giles. Any one of the dozens of hands which were trying to grip his simultaneously could be understood to have torn the bracelet from his wrist.

The police were getting things under control. Mrs. Giles let the hand-kerchief unfold. Then, emptied of its desperately incriminating evidence, she replaced it in the pocket of her blouse.

It was at that moment that she saw Miss Ashley.

Even in the kaleidoscopic shift of faces it was not possible to mistake Miss Ashley's. The creature was back in the throng, about eight or nine rows away, but Mrs. Giles with her willowy height could see her easily. Miss Ashley wasn't looking at her. She was looking at Kent, where Kent and Mayor Saltensburg were standing at the microphone.

Mrs. Giles saw Kent's answering look. Saw the careful mask that settled on his face. Saw the faint, the slightest gesture of warning which he sent to Miss Ashley before he turned and gravely gave his full atten-tion to Mayor Saltensburg's opening remarks.

Mrs. Giles felt sick. The flush, the joy over Kent's having been aboard the train was at ebb. Of course Miss Ashley would have put him up to that simplest of all deceptions from her stuffed bag of tricks. Last night she would have advised him to take a train back down the line and so be able to appear aboard the proper one this morning. These things, these heart-torturing things, were true. Because of the identification tag which had lain beside the dead man's hand and which was lying now on the platform at Mrs. Giles's ice-chilled feet.

Finally it was done.

Mayor Saltensburg escorted her and Kent to the door of the brougham and saw them inside. He kept the door open while he elaborated on the reception slated for the following afternoon at five—a little speech—nothing formal, just a brief resume by Lieutenant Giles covering his experiences in the South Pacific. Lieutenant Giles would know.

Then Miss Davis was at the door of the brougham and saying: "You'll be needing this, Kent. One of our brightest cops just picked it up on the station platform."

Kent took the bracelet and identification tag from her hand. Mrs. Giles caught the faint, sharp constriction of the muscles about his lips. She saw his eyes move swiftly, searching the sidewalk crowd. She saw, again, Miss Ashley.

"Thanks, Dawn," Kent said.

But he wasn't saying it to Dawn Davis. Mrs. Giles knew. He was saying it to that woman back in the throng, attributing to Miss Ashley the swift wit of having recovered that circumstantially threatening clue and of having shifted it to where it could be harmlessly found.

The brougham moved. The sun shone very brightly. Noise dimmed and, except for the clopping of the roached black mare, shortly the world was still.

CHAPTER 13

Kent shoved the bracelet and identification tag into a trouser pocket. "Must get the catch fixed," he said. Then a little of the tension left him and he relaxed back against the cushion. "This is very good. I've thought of this many times. Used to dream about driving along again with you, Grand'Mere."

Madame Lecloche, his French governess, had taught him to call her that. He had always done so, rolling the first r a little as Madame Lecloche had told him to.

"For how long will it be, dear?"

"Until Friday. I get that thing pinned on me then. Afterward they put me in a glass case and exhibit me around the country at the different plane plants. Buy a bond and you get a look. I don't know. It's good to be home."

"You're tired."

"Very."

"You'll find things changed. So many of them."

"Naturally. I gathered from your letters that none of the old crowd is left. Only palsied zanies and the lollipop set." Mrs. Giles smiled warmly. Surely during the brief quarter of an hour of the drive to the house she could force herself to impound all things within her hidden mind except for the blessing that Kent was beside her.

"Well, at least you gathered something," she said. "I got nothing whatever from your last note beyond the frightening assurance that you no longer could speak English. What *are* boon dockers?"

Kent's laugh was sudden and fresh. It cracked the strange hard glaze of his face entirely, making him look young again. "They're field shoes."

"And a gizmo?"

"A machine gun usually, otherwise it's anything you can't think the name of. What else?"

"Happily, dear, I have forgotten the others."

But it was no use. Mrs. Giles checked herself from going on. How could she keep her voice quite normal and tell him, as she had been on the point of telling him, of the changes at River Rest, of the defense workers whom he would find installed?

How *could* she break this news naturally when she knew it would come as no news at all? That he already knew. That Miss Ashley, during their fateful rendezvous last night, had told Kent how things were? And still, if this wall of pretense were to be kept up, this assumption of ignorance which curtained a heart-wrenching barrier between them, she would have to tell him before further minutes passed. It was about as hard a job as Mrs. Giles had ever had to face.

"Oh, Kent dear"—she said it brightly—"I've gone completely insane according to both Hopkins and Ella."

"Good. What brand? Is it the Mary-Queen-of-Scots complex or do you just see things?"

"No, dear. Either of those would be simple. I've rented our four guest rooms to defense workers."

(How surely only yesterday she had felt that Kent would understand her gesture, so much better than Papa ever could have. That he would receive this news, which now was not news, with enthusiasm, and what fun they would have in talking it over. How dead, how ash-like the words had become.)

Kent's astonishment was very forced.

"Tell me about it."

So Mrs. Giles did. She forced her way through the whole hollow story. It carried them to the gates.

"Lord, what a mess," Kent said, eyeing the uncut lawns.

"I know. Joel did make a try at keeping them mowed, but it was far too much. He's very old. It's so good of him to do anything at all."

Kent stuck his head out of a lowered window.

"The house looks fine. That hasn't changed."

Mrs. Giles could see nothing but the nape of his neck with its close-cropped, blue-black hair. Were his eyes flicking the shrubbery? Would that dear, bronzed hand gripping his knee ever relax again?

Kent pulled his head back in.

"Your night-shift roomer must be loose," he said. "I thought you told me his daytimes were for sleep? Anyhow, there's a fine specimen for a Grade-A chiller parked in a bathrobe on the porch."

"Oh dear. It must be Mr. Parling."

"Better get Hopkins to frisk him every time he enters or leaves the house."

The brougham stopped.

Kent helped her down, and Mrs. Giles's eyes traveled from leather bedroom slippers up along a Jacquard dressing gown to the man's completely (how certain she had been that it would be!) dead-pan face. Kent declined Hopkins' offer to take his kit bag in, and the brougham rolled off to the stables. The man took a slender cigar from a pocket and bit its end off cleanly with dazzling teeth.

"Mrs. Giles? Your maid fixed me up with a room this morning. I'm Parling."

"This is my grandson, Mr. Parling. Lieutenant Giles." Parling shook hands.

"Better help your grandmother inside, Lieutenant," he said. "The county prosecutor is in the parlor. They found a dead man under that bush."

Mrs. Giles did not have to call on artifice in order to blanch. Neither, she noted desperately, did Kent. The rich bronze tones of his cheeks were fading. She slipped a hand firmly under his arm, not for support but from an invincible desire to protect him. And from this wanting of hers to give him strength she found strength of her own.

She looked at Mr. Parling unflinchingly.

"Would you tell me, please, what happened?"

Parling lighted the cigar.

"Someone who came here looking for a room shoved his bicycle back a ways into the bushes and almost parked it on the body. He yelled like hell and it woke me up. This was around ten o'clock." Parling looked at a wrist watch. "Just two hours ago. I called the police."

"Who was it?" Kent asked.

"The stiff? Nobody knows. They dope it out as a simple case of mugging. There is plenty of that stuff going on around town, Lieutenant. You want to watch out if you're alone at night. Fat pay checks, fat pockets. Result, muggings. Bound to be. Have a cigar?"

"No, thanks."

"Nice place you've got here, Mrs. Giles. Nice view."

"Thank you, Mr. Parling. Papa chose the site because of that vista of the river. Naturally the town has encroached on us greatly since the days when Papa built."

"I think," Kent suggested, "that if the county prosecutor is waiting?"

"Of course, dear."

Parling flicked his cigar.

"He was talking things over with that maid of yours when I came out onto the porch."

"Oh dear! Leila?"

"Yes. She strikes me as something of a character. Is she all there?"

"Most of her is. She is my gardener's niece and—well, just a little vague."

"I see. Hard to anchor her."

"Coming in with us, Mr. Parling?" Kent asked.

"No, he's finished with me. There was nothing I could tell him. I'll just do a job on this cigar out here and then run up to bed again."

CHAPTER 14

Kent and Mrs. Giles went inside.

She could almost touch this wall which was solidifying between them with its texture of secret knowledge. She found herself unable to say a thing. She could neither marshal nor force out any of the normal comments which a woman, beneath whose azalea shrubs the corpse of a stranger had recently been found, would of a certainty make. But, then, neither could Kent.

In this stillness which was strange to the point of being almost a mutual admission Kent set his kit bag down in the hall and then followed his grandmother into the long, cool drawing room.

A man stood alone before a window at the room's southern end, looking out upon what had once been a charming rose garden. He turned and faced them. He was a well-built, large man in his early forties, with dark russet hair and with a general aura of almost rocklike reserve and imperturbability. Mrs. Giles felt instantly that he would be *dependable*.

"I'm Russell Stedman, Mrs. Giles. The county prosecutor."

Mrs. Giles held out her hand. She hoped that its tremors would be put down by Mr. Stedman to the reputed palsies which people so unpleasantly took for granted with women of her years.

"This is my grandson, Mr. Stedman. Lieutenant Giles."

Stedman shook hands with Kent.

"Sorry you had to have such a home-coming," he said.

"Thank you, Mr. Stedman. Just what did happen? Mr. Parling tells us the police thought it a mugging."

Stedman's smile was pleasant, but it held no humor.

"We think it best to let it ride for a while at that. Possibly for good. We tried to clear the decks as much as we could before you reached the house."

"That's very kind of you, but why?"

"The town is proud of you, and we want your leave with us to be a happy one. Don't worry about publicity. It won't rate even an item with any of the press services, and the *Gazette* will hold it down to a line or two on an inner page. The reception for you tomorrow will take over the front one." This, Mrs. Giles thought, is all too easy. It doesn't ring true.

Under their surface glossing they'll be working. A glossing not because they are stupid or willing in any sense to ignore their duties toward a murder, but for Kent's sake, and Washington, for the service, for the governor's presence at tomorrow's reception, so many important things.

"You'll probably want to freshen up a bit," Mr. Stedman was saying to Kent. "I always do after a train trip. I'll just chat with your grandmother while you're doing it. Then we can all run down and take a look at the body. I'm sorry it's necessary, Mrs. Giles, but that's one thing we have to do, find out whether you or anyone in the house can recognize it."

"I understand perfectly, Mr. Stedman."

"Your cook and maid and Mr. Parling saw it here before they took it away. None of them knew the man. The boys are getting in touch with Smith and Wade and Miss Ashley out at the works. We'll probably run into them down at the morgue." Stedman smiled again at Kent. "Take as long as you like, Lieutenant. No hurry at all."

Mrs. Giles waited until Kent had gone. She had observed his hesitation, his feeling that he should stay there with her, but she had smiled at him serenely and conjured up the insistence that he could do with a shave.

"Do sit down, Mr. Stedman."

Mrs. Giles selected an armchair with her back to the light.

Her favorite novels had well taught her the tactical advantages of this. She held no illusions about the coming chat with the county prosecutor. She sensed, as he took a chair facing her, that his imperturbability was simply an effect to mask his sharp interest while he obliquely fished his way through whatever streams he might decide she offered.

"There are a few confusing things, Mrs. Giles. Tell me, did you hear anything during the night?"

"No." Then she remembered her unhappy predicament in Miss Ashley's room. Miss Ashley, when questioned, might surely refer to it. "That is, not outside the house, Mr. Stedman. Inside, yes. A sound as though something had fallen in the hallway."

"You were in bed at the time?"

"Yes, it would have been around midnight. I went down the hall and knocked on Miss Ashley's door, thinking she might have stumbled, being unfamiliar with the house, but she was in bed."

"Did you find that anything had fallen?"

"No, everything seemed perfectly all right. I realized after returning to my room that it was nothing unusual. Frequently there are sounds. This is such an old house."

"Yes, I know the houses of this vintage. I referred of course to sounds outside, specifically down on the driveway. There are two ways of looking at it, you see. Three, really."

"I'm afraid I don't."

"No, naturally. One is that the man was stabbed out on the public road near the gate and that he ran in here to get help. He got as far as the shrubbery and then tumbled back into it and died."

"And the other possibilities, Mr. Stedman?"

"They both involve his having been stabbed while he was inside the grounds, probably close to where he fell. Possibly he realized he was being followed and ran in here to escape his assailant and, again, just got as far as the azaleas. I don't like that very much."

"No?"

"No, because I think in that case he would have yelled for help when he felt his assailant closing in on him. You would have heard the yell."

"Easily."

Mr. Stedman looked down at his thumbs.

"The third possibility involves a woman."

Mrs. Giles controlled her voice admirably.

"Woman?"

"Yes. The police feel there may have been a woman with him. There were certain indications which make them think so. They figure that the two of them may have strolled into your grounds last night, and some thug who had been following them stabbed the man, and that the woman then ran out on him in panic. Just left him there to die."

"Do they—might they not believe that this woman herself could have stabbed him?"

"They're not overlooking that. But they prefer the other. They like it better as a mugging. Maybe they'll catch up with the woman in time. They can tell about things better then." Stedman smiled suddenly and became very human. "I wonder whether you realize quite what a chance you took?"

Shock for a moment held Mrs. Giles rigid.

"Chance, Mr. Stedman? In what way?"

"By plunging into renting your rooms like this. In an ordinary house it wouldn't matter, or to a woman who is experienced and knows what she's up against. You don't. Really, the things I could tell you. You haven't any idea."

"No, I suppose I haven't."

"Your four roomers being in defense plants is a break, of course. Even to get their jobs they needed birth certificates and a clean dossier practically from the cradle on up. The police are looking into them out at the shops. If there is anything irregular they will let you know."

"That is most thoughtful."

Stedman stood up. He moved to the window and again looked out upon the rose garden.

"One of the reasons they think a woman was with him is a small shred of pale blue silk. They think it was torn from the sleeve or some part of a woman's dress which caught on the azalea bush. They argued for a while about its perhaps having been hooked there this morning when that mob showed up looking for rooms."

Stedman left the window and came back to Mrs. Giles.

"That bunch all had bicycles. I can't picture a woman wearing a pale blue silk dress on a bicycle. I look at it as the sort of dress a woman would wear at night," he said.

CHAPTER 15

Leila sifted through the doorway and toward them, while Mrs. Giles caught the touch of resignation which settled on Mr. Stedman's face.

"Yes, Leila?"

"Ella says you're to go right in and have your breakfast and that Mr. Kent is to have his too." Leila swerved mystic eyes toward Stedman. "Don't you dare try to stop them."

Stedman mentally mopped his brow.

"I won't. By all means have breakfast, Mrs. Giles."

"You will join us?"

Mrs. Giles sent Leila up for Kent. She took off her jacket and gloves. She led Mr. Stedman into the dining room, and Kent joined them as Leila brought in an omelet and broiled kidneys.

She gave but token attention to the talk between Kent and Mr. Stedman. It revolved largely around the war and the political aspects of postwar days. She was feverishly busied with the personal problem raised by the scrap of pale blue silk.

Mrs. Giles had no doubt but the scrap had been torn from the wrapper she had worn last night. The wrapper would have to be disposed of. In the furnace? Mrs. Giles had never started a furnace fire in her life, but she imagined there would be nothing difficult about doing so, any more than there was to applying a match to the kindling of a grate. But burning cloth smelled. Would its odors permeate the house and cause dangerous inquiries? Wouldn't burying the wrapper be best, in some ragged bed of the no-longer-cared-for gardens?

On the whole Mrs. Giles thought that such interment would prove the wiser course and decided to attend to it that night. She permitted the discussion to continue between Kent and Mr. Stedman without comment or interruption while they finished eating.

She went upstairs, ostensibly to put on her jacket and gloves. Actually she wanted to determine whether it really was her wrapper from which the scrap of silk had been torn. She thought how fortunate it was that the scrap's discovery must have been made almost within the hour, before suspicion would have been directed within the house and before Mr. Stedman or his associates would have made any search.

The wrapper was on its hanger where she had placed it last night. She took it from the wardrobe. Yes, in the right sleeve a bit had been torn out. Where to leave it between now and its later burial? That splendid story of Poe's occurred to her: *The Letter*. Or was it Gaboriau? It didn't matter. Swiftly Mrs. Giles got out basting thread and a needle, then she basted the incriminating wrapper inside of a long evening dress and hung it back on the rack.

Satisfied, she returned downstairs.

The postwar political discussion between Kent and Mr. Stedman ran on unabated after they were seated in Mr. Stedman's car, which he had parked by the stables, and were en route to the morgue.

The thought of visiting the town's mortuary held distaste for Mrs. Giles but no terrors or revulsions. She viewed the facade of a plain cement building as the car drew up to the curb.

Mr. Stedman and Kent flanked her as they went inside and entered a small reception room which in addition to a white-coated attendant and an unimportant-looking little man seated at a desk held Mr. Smith, his handsome young nephew Fergus Wade, and Miss Ashley.

Miss Ashley.

Mrs. Giles swiftly absorbed Miss Ashley's daytime armor: admirably cut dark slacks, a turtle-neck sweater, and a jacket of the same material as the slacks. Mrs. Giles had been unable to absorb the perfection of this outfit during her glimpse at the station. All she had then been able to see had been Miss Ashley's equally perfect (for its purposes) head.

"Well," Mr. Stedman was saying, "I see we're all here. Lieutenant, I don't believe you've met Mr. Smith and Mr. Wade. And this is Miss Ashley."

Mrs. Giles grew sick at heart as she eyed this fictitious meeting. Miss Ashley positively swiveled up to Kent and held out her hand.

"Hello there, Lieutenant."

"Hello, Miss Ashley. Glad that you're with us out at the house."

"Well, it's beginning to have its compensations."

Mr. Smith came over and forthrightly told Mrs. Giles how sorry he was that she would have to face this ordeal. She considered how solid, how substantial his work clothes made him look and how equally effective were those of his young nephew. Both men reminded her of the splendid posters depicting Labor at the forefront of the fight.

Then her eye was diverted by a look which passed between Mr. Stedman and the unimportant-looking man at the desk. Oddly it struck her as being one of secret significance. It made her suspicious of some possible official trickery and put her instantly on guard.

As they all followed Mr. Stedman and the white-coated attendant from the room she made certain that her hand was firmly fixed in the crook of Kent's arm.

"A shame your having to do this," Kent said.

"I don't mind."

"Anyhow, this will be the end of it."

"Of course."

But it wouldn't be. Mrs. Giles knew and felt that Kent must know so too. She held herself beside him when they stopped in a vault-like room filled with the pungent odor of disinfectant. They were grouped near a drawer-like slab on which rested the outline of a body beneath a sheet.

She saw the white-coated attendant step to the sheet and take hold of its upper end. She was aware that Mr. Stedman had moved to a position from where he could study the reactions that might come to their several faces. This is where we get it, she thought grimly.

They did, all right.

The attendant lifted the sheet. Mrs. Giles felt the muscles of Kent's arm contract against her fingers as her own heart skipped a beat. The exposed face was not that of the man who had lain dead beneath the azaleas. Mr. Stedman's trick at once became apparent to her in its full cleverness. If guilt lay among the observers shock might force it involuntarily to cry out: "That is not the man."

Silence held for a terrifying moment, and then Mr. Stedman said casually to the attendant: "You've pulled out the wrong slab, Jim." He turned to the rest of them. "I'm sorry to prolong this. That isn't the body. Jim missed the slab."

So she was right. Tricks had been planned. Mrs. Giles's belief was now solidly clinched that mugging as a motive might set all right with the police but not with Mr. Stedman. Mr. Stedman definitely linked the murder with River Rest, and beneath his air of agreeable sociability he was out to get them.

The slab slid in and the slab beside it slid out, and again a sheet end was raised.

Yes, Mrs. Giles thought, it's he. The face was sharper, clearer than it had been in the moonlight, making more prominent the diplomat, the foreign-court look. There was complete dignity on the face and utter peace.

A strangled cry shocked her severely.

"I got to get out of here," Mr. Smith's handsome young nephew said. His face was drenched with sweat and had turned the color of oyster shell. "I'm going to be sick."

CHAPTER 16

Mr. Stedman drove Kent and herself back and left them at River Rest. It seemed to Mrs. Giles that a century had passed before she found herself at long last in her sitting room and taking off her jacket and hat. Kent had said that he was going into his room for a rest. She knew only too well how greatly he needed one.

The most disturbing remembrance about their departure from the mortuary was the moment when Miss Ashley had said to Kent: "I'll be looking forward to seeing you out at the house this evening, Lieutenant."

Mrs. Giles still shuddered at the sultry, the provocative brazenness which had timbred Miss Ashley's voice. But she shuddered even more so at what had been Kent's reply: "I'll look forward to it too. Possibly, if you're not too tired from your work, we could chase up a dance or something in town."

Feeling a little faint, she sat down. She was too sodden with sheer worry, too filled with despair at the intricacies of this mess she was plunged in even to cry. And brokenhearted with fears for Kent. The ordeal at the mortuary had unnerved her more than she had imagined.

She frankly admitted that she didn't know what to do. Talk openly to Kent, she supposed. Nothing else, no other *sensible* course seemed left her. But not in this condition. First that panacea of all panaceas: a warm and nerve-relaxing bath. Mrs. Giles stood on weary feet and started for the bedroom door.

She opened it and stepped in and saw Leila. The girl stood facing the dresser. She whipped around on hearing the latch click, then swiftly concealed a hand while her eyes and features settled into a bland composition of sweet innocence. Mrs. Giles sighed.

"Give it to me, Leila. Whatever it is."

"I don't know what you mean. I'm sure I don't. I've just been finishing with straightening up your room."

"Whatever you've taken, dear."

"I don't take things. You might just as well accuse me of being a thief. Sometimes I just borrow something just to admire it. There's a big difference. A special one."

"Leila, I am a little nervous. Give it to me at once, please."

"I told you this morning you looked terrible. And now you look worse. You ought to see a doctor."

"I am not ill. I am fatigued. The demonstration at the station tired me."

"It was before you went to the station that I told you how poorly you looked. Mr. Stedman was just as worried about you as I was."

Mrs. Giles stiffened perceptibly. She could not vision the county prosecutor losing his imperturbability over a migraine.

"Mr. Stedman, Leila?"

"Yes. We had quite a talk before you and Mr. Kent got here."

"You discussed—me?"

"We discussed everybody. He seemed to want to. I told him you were so weak when you went out for a breath of air before breakfast that at times you had to steady yourself by putting a hand on the bushes."

"Did Mr. Stedman comment, dear?"

"Well, he was ever so interested and wondered whether you always took a stroll before breakfast. You don't, of course. As I told him. Honestly, you're just being stubborn if you don't see a doctor. Your face is perfectly white again." Mrs. Giles spoke with unaccustomed asperity.

"We will discuss it no further, Leila."

"Oh, very well. Here. Take it if you want it."

Leila, emulating the speed and intangibility of light, dropped a silver thimble into Mrs. Giles's hand and was no longer in the room. Even the door had been silent in its swift closing.

Mrs. Giles placed the thimble back on the dresser. It was the one she had used while basting the blue silk wrapper beneath the dinner dress. She never knew what would strike Leila's fancy. Sometimes the objects would be new and at other times they might have been lying around the house since the day when Joel had brought her.

She pressed finger tips upon the woodwork to steady herself. Mr. Stedman was anything but a dolt, and Leila's account to him of the pre-breakfast stroll with the pressing among the bushes surely would have registered in italics. The net which he was settling so gently about their shoulders would surely, soon, begin to be drawn in. It was utter madness not to talk with Kent at once.

She went out into the cool, dim hallway and rapped lightly on Kent's door. She waited for a moment before rapping again, then as there was still no answer she opened the door and went inside.

Kent was lying fully dressed on the bed, lost in deep sleep. A slant of sunlight curved his check, and Mrs. Giles's eyes were helpless with sudden tears at the youthful look of childlike innocence which sleep had brought him: all care wiped away. She walked to the windows and drew down masking shades, tempering the room into twilight, and then stood for a while by the bed.

She pictured in this sleep of deep exhaustion the endless quality which must have been his desperate night: awake through all of it after that grim rendezvous with Miss Ashley, waiting in dim stations for trains, beset with cares so deep and private that he would not share them even with her.

In danger surely.

In danger both last night and now. If Miss Ashley's *had* been the hand which had stabbed the stranger how increasing might become her reluctance to permit this witness to her deed to live. It was the commonest of gambits: these later murders grasped at as safeguards against knowledge of a deed already done.

And if the murderous hand belonged to someone else entirely?

Then surely the threat still obtained. The threat from the stranger who would have witnessed the victim fall as the result of his knife thrust, who would have witnessed the rendezvous between Miss Ashley and Kent, and who would dread that either of them might in turn have caught sight of him.

Not for an instant did it strike Mrs. Giles that she herself would also fit within that classification: that this hidden unknown might as easily have observed her own performance in the moonlight as he had Miss Ashley's and Kent's.

Kent stirred and she cursed her folly at having ever conceived this rooming refuge for war workers in the first place, no matter how essential and patriotic the idea might be.

How miserable it was that Kent's eagerly awaited homecoming should have turned out like this. Not only his military career but his life was in jeopardy of being warped by it. If the blaze of Miss Ashley's allure had blinded him into a truly desperate infatuation.

There would be no warping. Mrs. Giles vowed it. Not if she could help it.

"Sleep," she said quietly. "Sleep."

The telephone was ringing when she returned to her living room.

A man's voice said when she answered it: "This is Russell Stedman, the county prosecutor. May I talk with Mrs. Giles, please?"

Her hand pressed swiftly against her heart.

"I am Mrs. Giles, Mr. Stedman."

"I hope I haven't disturbed you. Will it inconvenience you if I borrow your coachman for half an hour or so?"

"Hopkins?"

"Yes. Stupidly we've just realized that he hasn't taken a look at the body. I'll run out and drive him down to the morgue if I may."

"Certainly, Mr. Stedman. I will see that he is ready."

"Thank you very much. I'll be out in ten or fifteen minutes. Say about three o'clock."

"Mr. Stedman—"

"Yes, Mrs. Giles?"

"I—naturally I am interested—but were there no papers or anything in his pockets? It seems so odd, especially nowadays when people bulge with classification numbers and ration books."

"No, no wallet, nothing. That is more or less to be expected in a mugging. Picked clean. We'll have a report on his fingerprints from the central bureau in Washington pretty soon. If they're listed that will settle it. If not—well, it won't be the first time we've been left holding an unidentified body. How is that grandson of yours enjoying himself?"

"Kent is sound asleep."

Stedman laughed pleasantly.

"That's what most of the boys seem to want when they get home on leave. Sleep, beefsteak, and, believe it or not, chocolate-ice-cream sodas. Well, thank you, Mrs. Giles. I'll pick up Hopkins in a quarter of an hour."

Mrs. Giles replaced the receiver. She pressed the button on the house telephone marked "Stable." She told Hopkins, when he answered it, that Mr. Stedman would call for him at three and what for. She asked him, when he returned, to let her know.

This stream which despite its gentleness kept moving so inexorably on! Now adding Hopkins. There was nothing which Hopkins could know.

She turned the water on in the tub.

CHAPTER 17

Stedman drove slowly.

He took in Hopkins obliquely. What, he wondered, were the chances of getting even one drop of value from this well so obviously dried into aridity by the years?

"Do you sleep in the house or over the stables?" he asked.

"In the house, Mr. Stedman. Ella, my wife, has a room with Leila. I have one of my own. All are on the top floor. Mrs. Giles thought it better for Leila to have a companion." A guard, Stedman thought, would be a happier word.

"Is the house noisy?"

Hopkins was somewhat affronted.

"Noisy?"

"I mean in the way that old houses usually are. Creaks and things. Rattling shutters."

"Not River Rest, Mr. Stedman. It was soundly built, and time hasn't affected it. Why, at nights you could hear a pin drop."

Oh, could you now? Stedman filed that away. He was bemused at the professional manner in which an undoubtedly sterling character such as Mrs. Giles could lie once she put her mind to it. He found himself feeling increasingly sorry for her. And very sorry for her grandson. Well, there was no rush. He decided to stretch to its ultimate limit the charitable kindness of delay.

"Did you hear anything unusual last night?" he asked.

"No, but then I wouldn't. I'm a sound sleeper."

They drove for a while in silence.

"What is your own opinion of this?" Stedman said.

"Ella and I both have no doubt about what is at the bottom of it."

"Really? Tell me."

"It follows the general law of things."

"I don't think I understand that."

"I am speaking of an established environment and an established class. It is similar to chemistry, Mr. Stedman. A proper blend is harmless. But you introduce an improper outside force into the mixture and get an explosion. That is what has happened to River Rest."

"The new roomers?"

"Certainly, sir. Not only Mrs. Giles herself but her every surrounding have established a certain balance; you might call it an atmosphere of life. By doing what she did she not only opened River Rest to roomers; she opened it to attack."

Stedman wondered whether the old fellow might not have something there. It was a thought completely foreign to his own presumptions, but certainly it was worth some future consideration. Not much, though. Too lavish an accumulation of the coincidental became absurd: four roomers from a local war plant, a grandson from the South Seas via Washington, all coming to a common focus last night on a corpse from God knows where. Nonsense.

He drew up at the curb.

The same unimportant-looking little man still sat at the desk in the morgue's reception room, and the same white-coated attendant stood near the door. Stedman introduced Hopkins and said they'd take a look now.

Stedman had no expectations, but he wasn't overlooking any trick. He had been voted into the job of county prosecutor by never having done so. When they reached the room with the rolling slabs the same business of the wrong body was gone through with, but it got him no farther with Hopkins than it had with the other bunch.

He hoped Hopkins wouldn't keel over the way that handsome hulk Wade had. Funny about that. Something funny, anyhow. If the simple sight of a cadaver was going to throw him into a faint why hadn't the first one? Why wait for the second? Well, some people needed the old one-two. But *was* there any connection in it with Hopkins' theory?

The right body was rolled out, and Hopkins stepped closer to the slab to get a better view.

"Yes, Mr. Stedman. The face is familiar. There is that foreign look about it which struck me. Yes, sometime recently." Stedman stopped rocking back on his heels.

"Who is it?"

"Oh, I don't know that, but he is a man I've seen."

"Where?"

"On the street, I suppose."

Blast, Stedman thought, all twittering zanies.

"Are you sure it wasn't about the grounds at River Rest?"

"No, I'd remember if it were. We have so few people who come there. I'm certain it was on the street. I enjoy observing faces while I'm sitting on the box waiting for Mrs. Giles. She doesn't go out much, but whenever she does go to a store or to the hairdresser's I like to watch the people walking by."

"I wish you could be more definite about this."

"I wish I could. It was quite recently. I know that. I suppose it was either yesterday afternoon while I waited outside the exhibition hall during the bond sale, or else this morning at the station. You'll probably put me down for a muddleheaded old fool when I say that I've also a feeling that neither of those places was the one. It was somewhere else."

Stedman did put him down for a muddleheaded old fool, and no probably about it.

He said with repressed resignation, "Possibly it will come to you."

"Oh yes. Things often do. After I've slept on them." Stedman decided to be philosophical about it. He considered the advisability of putting a guard on Hopkins. If the old relic had seen the victim there was always the chance that the murderer had observed the old relic observing the victim. That was pretty farfetched.

"We will go back now," he said.

CHAPTER 18

Stedman wondered as they drove back toward River Rest if any good would come from trying to jog Hopkins' memory with an association of ideas. He also wondered whether the old fellow might not be one of those thorough nuisances who occur in droves during so many investigations, who imagine or deliberately concoct fictitious knowledge just to shove themselves into the limelight. He could check on that with Mrs. Giles right now.

He left Hopkins at the stables and then drove around the curve and parked at the front door. He rang the bell.

He kept his fingers crossed while he asked Leila whether she would find out from Mrs. Giles if it were convenient to see him. Leila failed to evaporate. She said that she would and asked him very rationally to wait in the drawing room.

He put his hat on a completely carved console table and walked into the drawing room. What these old houses didn't know! Generations had made private worlds of them. You didn't find it in the October-to-October apartment life that was lived today. Not this atmosphere which was sifted with a touch of arrogance and the sound assurance that if it wanted to it could tell plenty.

"Back again, Stedman? Well, good afternoon."

Parling had walked into the room. He was dressed in a good gray business suit and looked very scrubbed and fresh.

"I thought I might catch Mrs. Giles in here," Parling said.

"I think she'll be down shortly."

"That's good. Quite a fine old character, isn't she? I know the type. You'd think a slight breeze would bend them over backward, but it doesn't. Strong as oxen as a matter of fact."

"Anything new on the case?"

"The boys are working."

Parling's lips moved fractionally into a smile.

"How familiar that sounds."

"Muggings are always a pain in the neck."

"Yes." The smile perceptibly increased. It looked astonishingly derisive for such a little thing. "Muggings."

"You seem to have different ideas about it."

"No, not at all. It just occurred to me that you and the boys are handling the case with a trowelful of *savoir-faire*. That's a French expression I picked up from a slummer across the old man's bar."

Parling broke off as he saw Mrs. Giles coming down the long room toward them. Mrs. Giles said good afternoon and suggested chairs. She thought Mr. Parling greatly improved now that he was no longer in a dressing robe but properly clothed and wearing a very good suit. It destroyed a good deal the saboteur effect while replacing it with something just as adventurous but without any sinister implications. She could not put her finger on just what.

"I wanted to see you about my car," Parling said. "Do you mind if I keep it parked in the stables?"

Mrs. Giles saw no reason why he shouldn't. Her own cars had been kept there until the gasoline shortage had made her unshroud the victoria and brougham and buy the roached black mare. Years ago a cement flooring had replaced the original one which Papa had had put in of oak.

"I will tell Hopkins that you wish to do so, Mr. Parling."

"Thank you." Parling stood up. "You two will want to talk privately."

"No, nothing private," Stedman said.

Oddly, Mrs. Giles found herself hoping that Mr. Parling would stay. Now that she had removed, or at least partially shifted, him out of the role of Menace she drew a certain—well, it seemed silly to call it a sense of protection (but that was what it was) from the steely quality in him.

"Do stay, Mr. Parling," she said.

Parling sat down again.

"I had just asked Stedman whether there was anything new."

"There isn't," Stedman said. "Nothing of any value. I thought I'd just check with you about Hopkins, Mrs. Giles, while I was out here."

"Check? In what way?"

"I'll put it like this. Does he like to be important? I mean is he interested in shoving himself into the limelight?"

"No, I should say the reverse. He is a very retiring man. A very good one. Why?"

"So many people will say anything that comes into their heads if they feel it will draw attention to themselves. You run into it all the time handling criminal cases. It runs from stating they witnessed things which are entirely in their imagination to the whole hog of making a confession to the crime itself. Silly."

"*Surely* Hopkins—"

"No. I felt instinctively about him what you tell me. That he's quite reliable. He says he saw the man before."

Mrs. Giles breathed deeply. She saw a glint of interest break through the mask of Mr. Parling's face.

She said, "Who was the man, Mr. Stedman?"

"That's it. Hopkins doesn't know. It's just that he saw the face sometime recently and it impressed him because of its foreign look. He thinks it was at some time while he was sitting on the box waiting for you. Either at the bond sale yesterday or at the station this morning." Stedman smiled. "Then he thinks it was at neither, but at some other moment during the past day or two. How old is he, by the way?"

"Eighty."

"Well, he hopes it will come to him. He says such things sometimes do after he's slept on it."

"What good will it do even if he should?"

"Frankly I don't know. The only value might lie in there being something indicative about the locality."

Stedman did not elaborate. He stood up and said good-by, but he did not leave at once.

"I've persuaded the chief to put a patrol on this section," he said casually. "Your grandson being home will attract people. Also the publicity about your taking roomers. There is plenty of monkey left in the average citizen. They read or hear about something and they've got to take a look, even if the only satisfaction they can get is in staring at the outside of a house."

Then he left.

CHAPTER 19

Parling took a cigar out of a vest pocket and began the leisurely process of preparing to light it.

"Good man, Stedman," he said.

Mrs. Giles had momentarily forgotten that Parling was there. The continued casualness of Mr. Stedman's manner increasingly perturbed her. In her opinion the patrol he had so thoughtfully arranged was not so much to protect the section as it was to keep a close official eye on River Rest and on the people in it.

Specifically upon herself. How would this patrol affect her proposed nocturnal interment of the blue silk wrapper? It would not, if the man were to stay out on the public road, but the very fact of his official presence in the vicinity would place an added difficulty on the task.

She wanted to be alone and think, but habit forced her to accept this social moment which Mr. Parling evidently intended to indulge in. He seemed completely settled in his chair. He was even striking a match to light his cigar.

"Does cigar smoke bother you, Mrs. Giles?"

"No, not at all. Papa always smoked them. He distrusted cigarettes."

"My old man did too. He smoked a pipe. He owned a bar in New York down on South Street. Called it the Seven Seas. He was quite a character. A romantic, in spite of his looks."

"He is dead, Mr. Parling?"

"Yes, about ten years ago. They got him out back in the alley one night."

"How horrible! How terrible it must have been for your mother."

"Well, I wouldn't say that. She was gone a couple of years before it happened."

"Dead too?"

"No, Oregon."

Mrs. Giles observed Mr. Parling with a peculiar fascination. This was life in the raw. Literally her first firsthand view. What a life to have led. How splendid to have risen from it. For obviously he was risen. A solid worker in a splendid cause. Doing his share. She observed his competent artisan's fingers as they prepared to relight the cigar which had gone out. Suddenly she knew.

She was certain as to what Mr. Parling was: an undercover agent for the government, working in war plants to detect saboteurs.

How clearly it explained the flexible steel quality in him, and how perfectly the dead-pan look. It also explained his casual, almost callous attitude when he had announced the finding of the stranger's body when he had met them on the porch that morning. Habit would have inured him to such deaths by violence, almost the usual run of his daily tasks.

And he would have undertaken this riskiest of all jobs because of the death of his father whom he must have loved deeply or else he would never have been able to understand that he had been, beneath his bartender's covering, a romantic. Yes, Mr. Parling had become an undercover agent to avenge him.

"They," the ones who had lurked in the alley and killed him, would surely have been gangsters of the most vicious type, and Mrs. Giles quite easily saw a youthful Mr. Parling dedicating himself to a life which would encompass such villains' erasement.

She said impulsively, "You are interested in criminals, Mr. Parling?"

The faintest of starts convinced her that she was on the right track.

"Me?"

"In their apprehension and ultimate punishment?"

Parling took time to think this over.

"Well, just about as much as any ordinary citizen would be. Why?"

"It occurred to me because of your father's shocking death. That you might have cared to avenge it."

Parling studied her curiously. There was a bemused, almost a fond look in his eyes.

"There are some things that people can't talk about, you understand."

Mrs. Giles did understand. Perfectly. The very essence of his work was secrecy. How well she knew that once an undercover agent's mask was torn off his life wasn't worth a red cent. She felt confused and sorry at having asked such a leading question.

"You must forgive me. My mind is so occupied with the murder of that stranger. I feel there may be something important in what Mr. Stedman said. Something most important, really."

"Said about what, Mrs. Giles?"

"That business about Hopkins trying to remember just where he had seen the man before. About some value lying in there being something indicative about the locality. Do *you* have trouble about remembering things, Mr. Parling?"

"Never."

"No, you wouldn't. But I do. I'm like Hopkins that way. I know we drove to the bond sale yesterday and to the station this morning. I can't for the life of me think where else. And yet this is what annoys me. There *was* a somewhere else."

Parling stood up. He looked at his watch.

"Time to be getting on," he said. "Thanks for letting me use the stables for the car. Would you mind my advising you not to worry too much?"

"Worry? But I'm not."

"I think that you are. I can tell when people are worrying no matter how they try to hide it." Parling set his cigar down on cloisonné. "Don't."

He took a wallet from his pocket and permitted one side of it to flap down while he idly inspected the papers which were in the other half. It was quickly done, really, but it gave Mrs. Giles the opportunity for catching a glimpse of the small plaque of metal pinned to the flap which hung down. Then he put the wallet back in his pocket and picked up the cigar.

Parling said nothing further, but he looked into her eyes for a second before he turned and left the room. Mrs. Giles read the unspoken message easily which he had sent her: pity, and understanding, and perhaps a life preserver in the wind. Such things she read both in his look and in the glimpse he had so deliberately permitted her to have of the badge.

A chill took hold of her as she realized that Parling would now have to be added to the list of Mr. Stedman and the police: the list with which she would have to battle in her fight for Kent's defense.

CHAPTER 20

Mrs. Giles paused at Kent's door on the way to her rooms. She opened it quietly and looked in. He still slept. It did not seem to her that he had even moved. She shut the door and went on to her living room.

It was half-past four. She sat down in a chair at a window and tried to think of nothing at all. It was impossible. A barrage of involvements spattered her. She resigned herself to the one requiring the interment of the blue silk wrapper.

A fork spade would be best, from the shed near the stable where Hopkins kept the garden tools. During some hour of the night when all would sleep. One hoped. Somewhere among the delphiniums. It would disturb the tulip bulbs—but then... Could the surface mat of weeds be replaced? It would have to be. Nothing must show.

The telephone rang at five.

"Russell Stedman, Mrs. Giles," Stedman said when she answered it.

"Oh yes, Mr. Stedman?"

"I found several reports waiting for me at the office just now. Most of them deal with your roomers. I thought I'd relieve your mind. They're all right. The police have finished checking their records out at the plant as well as doing some telephone verification on their own hook."

"That is most kind. I appreciate it very much."

"Smith, Wade, and Parling pass with flying colors. Miss Ashley introduces the only fly in the ointment, and it's a very small one."

Mrs. Giles thought swiftly: If it were only to ease my mind about having these people in the house the police would have been satisfied by their check of the records at the plant. But the police went in for further telephonic verification of their own. It is more than my peace of mind they are interested in. It's the murder. And Miss Ashley...

"Would you explain about Miss Ashley, Mr. Stedman?"

"As I say, it isn't much. Her records at the Collins plant are perfectly straight. It is simply that she had been rooming with a Mrs. Aldershot before she moved to you. When she left there she gave Buffalo to Mrs. Aldershot as a forwarding address."

"How queer."

"Well, the police did think so for a while until they asked Miss Ashley about it. Her explanation was perfectly satisfactory. Some man had been annoying her, trying to date her up, and she decided to shake him off by giving Buffalo as a forwarding address to Mrs. Aldershot instead of your house. Her mother said Miss Ashley was frequently troubled like that."

"Mother?"

Mrs. Giles had never envisioned Miss Ashley as having a mother. In the usual having-a-mother sense, that is. Nor any sort of family. Such spies and adventuresses were always without family ties: lone women cruising the globe in solitude while in lethal pursuit of their prey. Somehow this mother touch made her think almost kindly of Miss Ashley for a moment.

"Yes," Stedman was saying, "her mother is a widow. Lives out in Cleveland. She's down on Miss Ashley's dossier as the next of kin. When the boys phoned her, Mrs. Ashley satisfied them entirely about her daughter. Quite."

(Something cryptic, Mrs. Giles decided, in that. Especially Mr. Stedman's emphasis on the quite.)

"Incidentally," Stedman was going on, "the central bureau in Washington has identified the corpse for us. His fingerprints are on record. Very much so. I won't bother you with all of his aliases, but his favorite seems to have been Agualdo Russdorff. It has a global smack. He was quite a lad."

"In what way, Mr. Stedman?"

"In many ways. I suppose you could list him as one of those nuggets labeled international crooks. He's down on the books for almost every crime except murder. His specialty was blackmail." Stedman paused. A deliberate pause. "That sort of changes the complexion of things, Mrs. Giles."

How well, how nerve-wrenchingly she knew it! No international crook with such a record would ever permit himself to become the victim of a mere mugging. He would be far too adroit from years of being constantly on the defensive for anything so naive as that. And so the police would reason. More pointedly than ever would their roads now converge on River Rest.

"Yes, Mr. Stedman, I suppose that it does."

"Well, don't worry about it. Good-by, Mrs. Giles."

Mrs. Giles, as she hung up, was getting thoroughly sick of having people tell her not to worry. Leila, Mr. Parling, and now Mr. Stedman. As if she could stop. As if, ever, she could feel serene again.

There was something Mr. Stedman had said. Something in connection with Miss Ashley which should have registered. A definite discrepancy. Now it was gone. Mrs. Giles's head was too steaming to attempt to recapture it.

She went to the wardrobe and picked out a handsome Paris number of plum velvet and jet.

Kent came in as Mrs. Giles was finishing the last hook. Sleep had made him a different person, a little maturer than the boy who had left her, but no longer the careworn, taut man he had seemed at the station. He carried several packages, and Mrs. Giles saw with gratitude that his eyes were smiling as well as his lips. He dumped the packages on the bed and kissed her soundly.

"Loot," he said. "The treasures of Egypt. For you."

She sat down on the bed beside the packages and busied herself with unknotting string until the tears which swam in her eyes had cleared. Not now, never during this happy moment, this true happiness which she felt so surely her grandson was sharing with her, could she bring herself to beg him to explain his part in murderous conspiracy and furtive flight.

Later, yes, but not now.

The presents warmed her heart with a warmth which she had believed it would never feel again. This sudden oasis of being happy went to her head almost like the time when Papa had given her by mistake a wineglassful of bourbon instead of port.

The things he had brought her, had *thought* of to bring her while he must have been going through that daily hell over southern seas, were wonderful: a scarab brooch, the lovely garden of a hand-woven silk shawl, a vial of attar of roses, a necklace of garnet, carnelian, and jasper.

"And what on earth, darling, is this?"

"That is a nose ring, Grand'Mere, worn by the Fifis in Upper Egypt. A Fifi, as you don't know, is the girl friend. Very fashionable. Wear it at your next committee meeting or while lolling in the victoria and you'll knock them flat. I certainly wish you would wear it at that reception tomorrow afternoon."

"*Oh, Kent!*"

"Well, it would help a lot."

They talked, but she did not know of what, and they went downstairs together, and she watched him glut himself with roast chicken and, after, with frosted devil's-food cake which had taken practically every grain of sugar in the house.

How happily, how marvelously was it like the days before he had gone away: a trancelike interlude which held solidly its warming joy until they left the table and went into the drawing room.

"Hi there, Lieutenant," said Miss Ashley.

Mrs. Giles almost literally felt frost forming on her skin. The creature (again motherless so far as Mrs. Giles was concerned) was standing beside a buhl table and daringly leafing through Papa's large, handsomely bound family Bible. She was no longer in slacks but wore an organdy dinner dress which Mrs. Giles was compelled to admit had been masterfully cut by a first-rate house. It gave the wretch an all but wickedly deceitful air of virginal innocence.

Mrs. Giles could have killed her.

"Hello there yourself, Miss Ashley," said Kent. "You are looking very fit."

"I thought so." She shifted the impact of her sultry eyes with their eye shadow of pale mauve to Mrs. Giles. "You want to be careful for the next few days what you do. Jupiter's not so hot. He's with the Moon in a nadir in the sign of Pisces. My advice to you is don't travel."

The frost moved from her skin into Mrs. Giles's voice.

"Would you explain what you are talking about, Miss Ashley?"

"Your horoscope. I got the date of your birth from that Bible. When I get time I'll work it out. But right now I'm not kidding, Mrs. Giles. You keep away from travel. Anyhow, until next week. How about slipping a disk on the juke box, Lieutenant? Your grandmother has a nice place here all right, but boy, does it wrap me in shrouds."

Mrs. Giles sank into a rose damask fauteuil. Miss Ashley's magic (black) still worked. Mrs. Giles could see its poisonous brew befogging Kent's normally lively eyes. She could see it in the manner with which he walked in a rosy daze to the cabinet that held his private selection of records, in the way he gathered Miss Ashley into an arm and melted into rhythm as some brazen creature started moaning blue. They floated as one, toward her and away from her, upon the fluid floral designs of Papa's finest Kirman-Lavehr carpet.

CHAPTER 21

Mrs. Giles with relief saw Mr. Smith and his nephew hesitating in the doorway, having been attracted there by the music. "Attracted" was an insult to the dictionary, Mrs. Giles decided as her eardrums shuddered beneath the timpani of a famous drummer who was not only trying to drown out the wind instruments but was succeeding very soundly in doing so.

During the comparative stillness while the drums ceased and a death-bed baritone took over Mrs. Giles said loudly: "Do join us, Mr. Smith. Won't you and your nephew come in?"

She watched them approach and did hope that their entrance would break up that intimacy of the dance, graceful though it was, and (Mrs. Giles was frank enough to admit it) of a propriety which would have put to shame some of the capers at the country club which she had witnessed.

Smith and Fergus sat down on a love seat near her chair, well filling it. Mrs. Giles's never-resting mind flashed back to Leila as again the breath-taking good looks of young Mr. Wade faced her.

"I do hope you have recovered from your shock this noon," she said to him.

"Shock? Me?"

"Yes, during that unpleasant visit to the morgue."

Fergus smiled ingenuously.

"I never saw a stiff before. I guess it was too much for me." He dug down and brought up from the curious recesses of his mind the tritest of often-read phrases: "Everything went black."

"My nephew," Smith said, "has had a little trouble with his heart. So many athletes do."

The music and the baritone expired, then Miss Ashley and Kent came over and offered greetings. In the heavy pause which followed their acceptance Mrs. Giles, probably for the first time in her life, felt at a social loss.

What conceivable conversational topic could she introduce which would fuse these differing elements into a whole and soften the set, expectant grin on Mr. Smith's rugged face, the smoky blankness of young

Mr. Wade's altar-boy eyes, the faint daze in Kent's, and that sultry *something* in Miss Ashley's?

She was almost grateful when Miss Ashley herself took the situation in hand. Hypnotized, she listened while Miss Ashley extracted the birth dates of the three men and then promptly proceeded to forecast their immediate futures.

"You," Miss Ashley said to Smith, "have a remarkable experience before you. Mars, the planet of force, is in the second house. Your experience will be concerned with finances. I advise you to go ahead with any plans you have in mind.

"You," she said to Fergus, "are strangely linked by the planets with the destinies of your uncle. The Sun and Venus are culminating in the sign of Virgo. And that means, my handsome friend, beware of skirts. So far as Fifis are concerned, my advice to you is to take a sabbatical."

That was perfectly agreeable to Fergus.

"Where," he said, "do I get one?"

"I'll let you know. As for you, Lieutenant, you are going to follow that cute suggestion you made at the morgue and take me out upon the town. I'm all for rug cutting, but not on a rug."

Mrs. Giles could see that this was not unpleasant to Kent, although it did occur to her that there was something overdone, a forced note in his enthusiasm. She wondered why. Especially in view of what had been his obvious, almost doting pleasure in Miss Ashley's company before Mr. Smith and his nephew had joined them.

Then she knew what it was: the enthusiasm was *acting*. Kent had always been the worst possible sort of actor. The kind which Mrs. Giles understood they called ham. She never had forgotten that ghastly moment while he was in boarding school when she had sat with such agony through Kent's interpretation of a sophisticated faun.

She assured him that she didn't in the least mind his going, especially as it was approaching her accustomed hour for retiring. She hoped that Miss Ashley and he would have a pleasant evening and said that she would breakfast with him at whatever hour he got up. She suggested a taxi instead of the brougham as Hopkins' retiring hour coincided with hers.

Miss Ashley paused at the doorway as they were leaving the room. She said, "Didn't something unpleasant happen to you back in 1928?"

How odd, Mrs. Giles thought. Because there had. That was the year in which she had almost died from a severe attack of influenza.

"Why, yes, Miss Ashley. I was seriously threatened with influenza. What made you ask?"

"I got that far in your horoscope." Her smoldering eyes moved lazily from Mrs. Giles to Smith and Fergus. "Smart guys, those stars."

Then she and Kent left.

Mrs. Giles watched their vivid young figures vanish into the gloomy hall. A chill shook her. How queer that Miss Ashley should have hit on 1928. Could there be anything in it? Could Miss Ashley, in addition to her perfect ability to control the present, lift the veil and forecast things to come? Then Mrs. Giles found herself somewhat taken aback at the flash of resentment she caught on Mr. Wade's face. But naturally it would be there: swift jealousy of Kent or of any man who would remove so gaudy a plum. That woman had an endless net.

Surprisingly Kent was back in the doorway, saying: "I've brought you the press," and bowing Dawn Davis into the room. He added: "Her finger was reaching for the doorbell."

And again he was gone.

Miss Davis looked brightly professional. She gathered up Smith and Fergus with a glance (the section swept at Fergus paused for a stopover) and said to Mrs. Giles: "I warned you, you know. I do hope you don't mind."

Mrs. Giles was at sea.

"Mind?"

"I said this morning that I would interview your guests. I seem to have missed Miss Ashley, thanks to Kent. I'm still wind-blown from the speed with which he whisked me past her."

Mrs. Giles clutched at her manners. She introduced. Miss Davis refused to take off her things.

Miss Davis sat down.

"I remember seeing you at the bond sale, Mr. Smith."

"And I am in your debt for having made it possible for my nephew and myself to be here."

"I also remember that when you looked at Mrs. Giles' etching you said that it reminded you of home. Was it Maine?"

"It was," Fergus broke in, "Long Island. My parents were blown up in their launch on the Sound."

"But how dreadful, Mr. Wade. You must tell me."

"I just did."

"My nephew," Smith said, giving his nephew an imperative look, "was a child of tragedy. He was seven. He has lived with me ever since. Our home, Miss Davis, was a simple cottage near the Hamptons. Frequently during the winter a deer or two would come to our pond, and that is why the etching meant so much to me."

"And now, do give me your reactions to River Rest."

Oh dear, Mrs. Giles thought, I *am* so glad Miss Ashley isn't with us to give hers.

Smith restrained a hurried look around the walls.

"I never knew," he said, "that such a place existed. Magnificent."

"And you, Mr. Wade?"

"Magnificent."

Miss Davis wondered whether or not she had enough. She thought she had. The exploding launch plus Mr. Wade's physique and the simple Hamptons cottage with its deer were good for several sticks. The quote "Magnificent" was a sufficient horse on which to drape her rags-to-riches angle. And there was still that Ashley vision to be chased through the town's three night clubs.

She stood up. She was furious at not being able to discuss the murder, but that had been clamped under an official taboo.

"This has been very kind," she said at large.

She said good-by. She started for the doorway. Hamptons? Sound? Why keep a launch on the Sound when you lived miles across the island on the other shore? It was a little thing, but Miss Davis wondered, as she left the house whether there could be something there. Discrepancies, however slight, could prove important when their perpetrators occupied a scene of crime.

CHAPTER 22

Mrs. Giles could feel a stolid sense of sympathy radiating toward her from Mr. Smith. There was nothing tangible about it, but she knew that it was there.

Her mind had the ability for tangents, no matter under what emotional stress (a good thing, of course, or currently she would have gone mad), and she suddenly thought how nice it would be if Mr. Smith's nephew would pose for an etching. Those perfect features done in cameo with just a suggestion, perhaps, of the sweep of Mr. Wade's superbly muscled shoulders and upper arms.

The tangent ended as she realized Mr. Smith was saying: "You have had a trying day. Fergus and I will wish you good night."

In this emptiness which had been left by Kent's departure with that creature, Mrs. Giles did not want Mr. Smith and his nephew to leave her. The last thing she felt she could bring herself to face would be an hour or two alone in her rooms, tormented with conjectures and harrowing thoughts, until the hour would come when it would be safe to bury the blue silk wrapper.

She cast about for a topic of mutual interest which might hold them.

She said: "They have identified the dead man."

It held them all right.

Mr. Smith, who had started to rise, fell back upon the love seat, and the oddest expression flashed over Mr. Wade's face while his splendid muscles tensed.

Wade got as far as: "What did I tell you?" when Smith cut in with an abrupt: "Who was it, Mrs. Giles?"

"I believe Mr. Stedman said the man's name was Agualdo Russdorff. That was his favorite one. His other aliases he didn't favor quite so much. The central bureau in Washington identified Mr. Russdorff from his fingerprints."

Smith immediately plunged into a sound lecture on crime. He covered its roots, its fruits, and the inevitable end which awaited all tasters of the same. Mrs. Giles warmed to him more than ever.

As he talked he reminded her strongly of that splendid and stanch Mr. Wattlestone who had made such an impression on her youthful mind in the calm little church she had attended with Mamma and Mademoiselle as a child. Their pew had been beside a window which was always open on Sundays, and the smell of catnip would come in. She would have liked to linger with this memory, but she forced her attention back to what Mr. Smith was saying.

He wanted to look at the studio. He thought that perhaps a quarter of an hour in the serene milieu of art would take her mind off the tragic happening of the morning. It struck Mrs. Giles as an excellent suggestion, and she led the way out into the hall and up the stairs.

Smith paused as they came to the door of his room.

"I wonder whether you would step in for a moment and let me show you something, Mrs. Giles."

"Certainly."

"I have made a slight alteration in the decorations."

He opened the door and switched on a ceiling cluster. Mrs. Giles went inside, followed by Fergus. She looked around. The room seemed the same. It was still the Blue Room. That was another fad Papa had blindly followed: decorating the four guest rooms each in a distinctive color.

For years Mrs. Giles had thought the Red Room pretty terrible, but she had never redecorated it because Papa had been most pleased with it of the lot. "Now that's a color you can get your teeth in!" he used to say.

"But I see no change, Mr. Smith."

"Look on that wall there."

Then she saw it. At the space where a water-color sketch involving blue sky and a beached rowboat with a blue hull had always hung. This trifle now was gone, and in its place Mr. Smith had put her etching of the thirst-quenching stag.

Mrs. Giles felt genuinely flattered and pleased. She said so, then she took them upstairs to the attic floor and into the room which Papa had had fixed over into a studio.

It was a large room with a long row of windows to let in the north light. There had been some talk of a real skylight, but the roof was mansard and weighty with slate, and Papa had felt it would spoil the looks of the place terribly.

A row of cupboards lined the east wall for her etching materials and supplies of paper while the Payne and Sons' Albion hand press, covered with a dust sheet, stood out in the room's center. She wondered idly what, if anything, Leila had added to her kleptomaniacal loot. For some time now Leila had been using one of the wall cupboards as a cache, and its contents, the last time Mrs. Giles had looked into it, had embraced such trifles as a copper ash tray, an egg beater, and a piece of costume jewelry.

As soon as the studio lamps were turned on Mrs. Giles knew that Mr. Smith was a true artist. There was a positive eagerness in the way he removed the dust cover from the hand press.

It seemed silly to say so, but his hands did have an almost fondling touch as they moved about and tested the condition of the press's mechanism. Even his nephew seemed to have caught a dash of Mr. Smith's suppressed air of pleasure, for he also was examining the press in a thoroughly interested fashion.

"It's in very good shape," Smith said. "Let me congratulate you, Mrs. Giles. Not many women feel such a responsibility toward machinery. But then you are an artist. Naturally you are sensitive regarding your tools. Would you think it presumptuous if Fergus and I were to take it apart and give it a thorough going over some evening?"

"I would be deeply grateful. Mr. Smith. In fact, I had hoped that you might care to join me in doing a plate or two."

"Splendid!"

"The thought occurred that your nephew might even consent to pose. Just the head and upper torso, say in cameo. Would you, Mr. Wade?"

Fergus glanced at Smith, who permitted an eyelid to lower briefly. So Fergus offered his shy smile and said he'd like to pose whenever Mrs. Giles wanted him to.

"If I recall correctly," Smith said to her, "didn't you tell Miss Davis at the bond sale about still having some of your original stock of India paper?"

"Yes, in fact, I've most of it. Both the India and bond. Papa bought me an awful lot. Papa always did buy much too much of things. It's in this cupboard, Mr. Smith."

Mrs. Giles opened the door of the cupboard which was farthest removed from the one where Leila had her cache. She felt most warmly gratified when Mr. Smith examined the large stock of paper with a nonplused respect which amounted almost to awe.

"How lucky you are, Mrs. Giles. This stuff is made from pure linen rags." He held a sheet against the light, then tested its flexibility and strength. He shut the cupboard door reverently, as though upon a gold mine. "It is impossible to get hold of paper like that today. You have no inks, of course. Not if you haven't done any etching for a good many years."

"No, and I'm afraid my stock of Dutch mordant may have deteriorated. It would have, wouldn't it?"

"That is according to how it has been kept, Mrs. Giles. I think it would be safer to get a fresh supply. I do hope you will permit me to attend to it, and also to the inks. I will feel I won't be imposing so greatly then for using your priceless paper and the press. Dear, dear, but this carries me straight back to the Academy. Such happy days. That carefree student life! "

For a full half-hour they talked shop. Fergus fiddled in fascination with the press, and Smith was most kind in his criticism of a folio of Mrs. Giles's India proofs which he persuaded her to show him.

Then they returned to the door below and said good night, and Mrs. Giles went into her living room. The pleasant half-hour dropped from her as she shut the door.

Her problems were with her again.

CHAPTER 23

Through the smallest of cracks Smith observed Mrs. Giles going into her living room, then he closed the door.

"I'm all of a sweat," he said to Fergus, who had come in with him. "A thing like that shakes me."

Fergus, with the unerringness of a homing pigeon, sought the bed and stretched out flat on his back. He flexed whipcord muscles and yawned, then his face took on the peculiar expression it assumed whenever he attempted to think.

"How soon do we clear out of here?"

"It will take at least a week, possibly two. And I suggest that you lower your voice."

"Come over close then."

Smith sat on the bed, choosing the foot of it in a desire to be as far away as possible from those strong, capable hands which Fergus was clasping under his neck. Funny how that thought was there whenever the fingers moved. Upsetting.

"That star stuff," Fergus said.

"Of Miss Ashley's?"

"Yes."

"The rankest rubbish. An amateurish attempt to focus attention upon herself. Even if she knew what she was talking about, which I doubt, there would be nothing to it."

"She told you to go ahead with finances," Fergus said flatly. "What's dopey about that?"

Smith drew his breath in sharply.

"So she did." His brows contracted. "Now I wonder."

"And I am to beware of skirts."

"That, of course, was absurd."

"Not if you look at it like this."

"Like what?"

"Like the fact that I know I've seen that skirt before."

"Miss Ashley?"

"Yes."

"Where? This could be tremendously important."

"I think it was the day you went to the bond sale. I think where I saw her was down by the shack."

Smith said with wretchedly controlled impatience, "Why in heaven's name haven't you spoken of this before?"

"Because I didn't think of it before."

"Wait here."

Smith got up from the bed. He went out into the hall and assured himself it was deserted. He slipped like a shadow through its melancholy light to the door of Miss Ashley's room and went into its darkness. He turned on a light.

Methodically for the next quarter of an hour he gave it a careful and thorough going over. Nothing escaped him and, when he was finished, everything was back in its place.

He put out the light and returned to his own room and to Fergus.

"Queer," he said. "There was nothing whatever of significance. That in itself is significant. Such initials as there were were correct, E. A., but there was no correspondence of any kind. No photographs. I think some personal research may be called for at the first opportunity."

"I'm worried."

"Well, stop it, and leave things to me."

"I like things quick. I don't like it here. I want to get out of here."

"I wonder if I can make you understand that, even if there should be anything a little unusual about Miss Ashley, it we were to leave here it would be the most foolish thing we could do. I mean even apart from upsetting the whole plan and delaying matters until it might be too late. Stedman is no fool."

Fergus' eyes grew smokier. A hot light played in them.

"Neither was Russdorff a fool. Much. You're not making sense. A week—two weeks—with Stedman pushing his nose around." The hands unclasped and one arm slid fluidly flat on the bed. The palm was up, the fingers gently curved. The palm was curiously deficient in lines. The plain of Mars was pronounced. A palmist would have been interested. "Where," Fergus said, "does that leave me?"

Smith sighed. One uses, he thought, the tools which are given to hand. It would be as futile to chide or to attempt to shape Fergus as it would be to mold the wind. But was he being fair? Could Fergus with his primordial slant on things be right, both about Miss Ashley as a questionable quantity and in his instinctive anxiety to get out of River Rest?

Smith wondered frankly whether he was not blinding himself because of the incredible perfection of the layout. No, he thought not. The rewards would more than cover any risks, even the gravest.

"You don't trust me."

A hint of embers smoldered through the smoke.
"I got to trust you," Fergus said.

CHAPTER 24

Mrs. Giles set the hand of her small traveling alarm clock for four o'clock. She had determined it as the morning hour most apt to find her world in bed and sound asleep, in that deepest sleep of the night. At its gentle, tuneful ringing she planned to arise and take care of that business of the blue silk wrapper.

As an aid to slumber she again took the fall of the Roman Empire with her to bed. She accompanied the son of Constantius while he conquered Maxentius at the Milvanian bridge in Rome and then, faced with a chatty but terribly learned dissertation on how he divided the empire with Licinius, she shut the book. The hour of the night was half-past twelve.

She put out the light.

Everything (but sleep) rushed at her through the darkness.

How correct she had been in her estimate of Miss Ashley as a creature of guile. In addition to Mr. Stedman's telephoned fly in the ointment that Miss Ashley had given Mrs. Aldershot Buffalo as a forwarding address instead of River Rest (not for an instant did Mrs. Giles swallow the trivial, excuse that Miss Ashley had done so to "shake off a man." That, Mrs. Giles thought grimly, would be the day), Mrs. Giles now distinctly recalled their first interview.

In it Miss Ashley had certainly announced herself to be a gun inspector at the Merle plant. Merle. Unmistakably it had been Merle.

Yet in spite of this, Mr. Stedman had said over the telephone that Miss Ashley's dossier had been checked at the Collins plant. And that was the plant where Mr. Smith and his nephew were enrolled.

Confusions piled on confusion. Miss Ashley and the two men had been strangers up to the moment when Mrs. Giles had introduced them in the drawing room. Or was this also a cut of duplicity to be stirred in with the rest of the noxious stew?

Surely in a war plant where thousands were employed Miss Ashley and the two men easily might never have met. It would be, she decided, like a crossing on any of the large liners where you reached Southampton and then saw dozens of new faces which you had never known were on board.

Nevertheless, it caused Mrs. Giles to pause on the lip of a read-justment of her extremely favorable impression of Mr. Smith and his nephew. But that was nonsense.

No sound in the silent house disturbed the eddied turmoil of her dark conjecturings. Hopkins stepped out from among them. Hopkins, seated on the box and waiting, and then impinging on his memory the foreign face of Mr. Russdorff. Where?

(*The only value might lie in there being something indicative about the locality*, Mr. Stedman had said.)

Mrs. Giles wondered in the room's crepuscular moonlight whether Hopkins, when he woke up in the morning, would remember. Suddenly, as such things occasionally would with her, it came in a flash. She knew where, within the immediate past, Hopkins had sat waiting on the box and had viewed Mr. Russdorff's face: at the end of Joroloman Street while he had waited for Mr. Smith and Mr. Wade to collect their luggage and bring it to the brougham from the tarpaper shack.

At no other time could it have occurred. With the exception of the bond sale and the railroad station, neither one of which Hopkins had felt to be the spot, his trip to pick up Mr. Smith and Mr. Wade to drive them to River Rest was the only other time when the carriage had stood waiting.

Good solid Mr. Smith and his dazzling nephew and, in their vicin-ity, the so-soon-to-be-murdered Mr. Russdorff. And the dazzling nephew had been thrown into violent illness when he had viewed, at the morgue, the proper corpse.

The only value might lie in there being something indicative about the locality.

Well, there was the locality all right. Plunk at the spot where had resided her two favorite roomers.

Mrs. Giles's stout heart all but flipped over. It was now for Hopkins that she was concerned. What the basis of the whole wretched affair might be she did not know. She felt immeasurably confused, and her belief that Miss Ashley had killed Mr. Russdorff was befogged by further doubts concerning Mr. Smith and his nephew because of Hopkins' hav-ing seen Mr. Russdorff near their shack.

It was tenuous; it was perfectly maddening, but Mrs. Giles consid-ered strongly that Hopkins was threatened with dangers from that simple thing. It still did not occur to her that similar, if not greater, danger was threatening herself.

She decided that nothing would stop her from talking with Kent the first thing in the morning. She would have gone in and talked with him right then, only she knew that he and Miss Ashley had not as yet come home. She had heard no taxicab crunching on the drive below.

Her eyes of their own volition closed.

They opened, still on darkness, to the gentle ringing of the alarm clock's bell.

She lay still for a while, testing the stillness of the house and of the world outside. Even the birds had not as yet begun their murmurous cheeps.

Mrs. Giles turned on a shaded lamp and got up.

She moved quietly through this sleeping world with planned determination. She pulled the bastings which held it beneath the dinner dress and put the blue silk wrapper on. Then over that she slipped another wrapper of black China silk. She was fully aware of the hazards of disposing of incriminating evidence. Almost invariably it was done up into a bundle which the disposer lugged about in full view, half the time to his frustration and ruin.

Mrs. Giles intended to have none of that. Should the worst occur and someone accost her, her hands would be innocently empty while the guilty wrapper would be safely concealed, and she would simply say that she had stepped out to investigate a suspicious sound. Let them make of it what they would. She could always, as a last resort, take refuge in her dotage.

She took a pencil flashlight from a bureau drawer and, after turning out the bed lamp, let its beam guide her through the quiet house downstairs into the kitchen. She selected the keys for the tool shed and the back door and stepped out into the night.

It pleased her to think that she had had the foresight to wear galoshes, as the dew on the grass was heavy. She stood still for a moment, accustoming her eyes to the crepuscular half tones brought out by the starlight, then took the path through the vegetable garden to the tool shed.

Inside this cluttered cubicle she used her flashlight sparingly to select the spade fork. She carried this with her to the erstwhile formal garden where, among the delphiniums, she dug a satisfactory hole. Nothing had alarmed her, and the darkness continued to offer its protecting screen.

She took off both wrappers and replaced the black China silk one before wadding the blue one into a ball and shoving it down into the hole she had dug. Earth was replaced and the surface smoothed with the fork's tines. She knelt and replaced as best she could the surface pad of weeds which she had set to one side. She thumbed it carefully down.

A shadow merged gently into the darker shadow of a lilac bush.

Mrs. Giles stood up. She took the spade fork and returned it to the tool shed, where she cleaned its tines with a burlap bag. She locked the shed and returned to the house. She carried a sense of victory with her upstairs to her rooms.

The shadow left the darker shadow of the lilac bush and went over to the delphiniums, where it kneeled.

CHAPTER 25

A brilliant sun rode high toward noon when Mrs. Giles opened her eyes. Leila was standing beside the bed. Leila was saying that Miss Dawn Davis was calling and had insisted upon Mrs. Giles's being awakened because of the parade.

Mrs. Giles remained groggy with sleep. Physically she felt tremendously refreshed, but her powers of concentration were still not all they should be.

She did her best to co-ordinate Leila's further statements that Mr. Kent had had to go down to the City Hall for a conference with Mayor Saltensburg on the reception for his official welcome to the town, and the hour for this had been set ahead from five o'clock to two, because of the governor's convenience, and although Mr. Kent would still get the key to the city there weren't going to be any cocktails.

Slowly Mrs. Giles got out of bed. She asked Leila to tell Miss Davis that she would be down soon. Her clock said half-past eleven.

The dregs of sleep cleared, and frustration hit her sharply. Her nocturnal activities among the delphiniums had caused her to oversleep to this hour when Kent had already left the house. So her frank talk with him was again delayed. It might even continue to be delayed until after the reception was over. She recalled the urgency she had felt last night because of Hopkins.

This morning, her head clarified by sound sleep, the threat to Hopkins took solid form. Precedents abounded: any number of times one of the characters would be attempting to remember something which, when recalled, would prove desperately detrimental to the murderer. The character would sleep. Sometimes in a hospital bed, sometimes in his own. And before his subconscious could shove the memory up to be seized by his mind on waking, the murderer would kill him. Thus sealing the secret in the tomb.

Which was precisely what Hopkins had been in the process of being last night.

Mrs. Giles hurried to the house telephone and punched the stable button. Relief flooded her as Hopkins answered it. "Good morning, madam."

"I'm so glad. Good morning."

"What was that, madam?"

"I will want the victoria earlier than we had planned, Hopkins."

"Yes, Leila told us that the reception was set ahead to two o'clock. I'll be ready."

"Thank you. And, Hopkins—"

"Yes?"

"Do you think the locality where you saw Mr. Russdorff could have been where you were waiting for Mr. Smith and Mr. Wade at the foot of Joroloman Street?"

"Yes. That's it. I remember his face being quite clear under a hanging bulb, sort of a makeshift street light. I'll telephone Mr. Stedman and let him know."

Mrs. Giles hung up the receiver. She continued to enjoy the relief which the sound of Hopkins' voice had brought her. She went to the wardrobe and wondered what on earth to put on.

Leila had definitely said a parade, which suggested some sort of official reviewing stand, and Mrs. Giles took it for granted that she would be invited to sit with Mayor Saltensburg and the governor.

The day promised to be warm, and she decided on a moderate version of a picture hat because of having to sit outdoors in the sun. She took from its box a nice one she had bought in London. It was very English. She thought it would be just right: that dowager-at-a-royal-garden-party note which Mayor Saltensburg would expect. Yes, it and the ecru lace dress.

She went down to the drawing room and found Dawn Davis in her usual state of surcharged excitement. Mayor Saltensburg. Miss Davis said, had sent her out to arrange things at this end with Mrs. Giles while he himself cooked the program up with Kent at the City Hall, and, my dear, you look exactly like a duchess heading for the strawberries and clotted cream.

Mrs. Giles smiled amiably.

"What are the arrangements, Miss Davis?"

Miss Davis said happily that the thing had got completely out of hand and was assuming the proportions of a whoop-de-doo on the scale of a *fête de grand luxe*. The newsreel services were taking it up. Their plan was to shoot Mrs. Giles and Kent as both stepped into the victoria at River Rest.

Mayor Saltensburg had originally planned that Kent would ride in the official car, but the movie people had insisted on the victoria idea from the moment when they learned that Mrs. Giles used a horse. Something to do with pounding home the conservation of gasoline.

Mrs. Giles repressed a shudder. She thought: Very well, if that is what they wish it to be. If that was how they wished to honor her grandson and to have him in turn do his service and the country the most good. To nourish that puzzling, that temperamental matter called morale.

"We will be completely at the mayor's service," she said.

Dawn Davis momentarily lingered.

"I missed them last night, Mrs. Giles."

"Missed?"

"Kent and Miss Ashley. I went to all three of our better tinseled sluicing premises, trying to run her down for an interview, but no dice."

Mrs. Giles, with a remarkable effort, retained her serene front.

"Perhaps they had decided to do their sluicing on some premises with less tinsel."

Miss Davis smiled briefly.

"Perhaps."

She stood up and thanked Mrs. Giles and said good-by. She left with her personal knowledge that there was no perhaps about it. She had searched for Kent and the Ashley creation on a descending scale through all the stews and cesspools of the town. With no result beyond a hangover which was piloting bulldozers about inside her head.

Mrs. Giles sat still and pondered this latest advice. Where had Kent and that poisonous product of a miasmic demi-world gone? To what dens (secreted even from the eyes of the press) had she lured him? She was unable to picture the sterling worthiness of Bridgehaven as possessing any dive so plushily and incense-ladenly apt. She gave it up.

The delphiniums.

It would be wise in this bright light of noon to view her handiwork. Mrs. Giles went out of doors. She made her way in leisurely fashion toward the garden, being careful (in case Leila were again observing the performance) to clutch at no bushes en route.

She paused and looked down at the spot where she knew she had dug. Nothing looked disturbed. No trace of digging showed. It had been a splendid job.

Splendid.

CHAPTER 26

The one-o'clock summer sun was bright and hot.

Mrs. Giles accepted Kent's hand and stepped into the victoria while cameras cranked. She thought that Hopkins seemed worried.

"Did you telephone Mr. Stedman?" she asked him while some close-ups of Kent were being shot on the drive.

"I couldn't get him, madam. A man at his office told me to call later this afternoon. He asked whether it was important and I told him no."

Like a cloud shadowing the bright sunlight, a wave of dread sifted over Mrs. Giles as her conviction increased that it *was* important.

"You look worried, Hopkins. Is it because you couldn't get hold of Mr. Stedman?"

"No, madam. It's the mare."

"Perhaps the confusion and these cameras annoy her."

"She was skittish while I was harnessing her."

The cameramen were finished with the close-ups, and Kent stepped into the victoria. Sleek and black and strong, the roached mare danced into a trot.

"She ought to be in the Ballet Russe," Kent said.

Mrs. Giles settled herself more firmly against the cushion. "I remember so many parades, dear. In almost all of them some stout official astride a white horse would land on the pavement before they were over. We are perfectly in style."

Mrs. Giles said it lightly, but a brief break which the mare made and which Hopkins adroitly controlled sent a tremor through her; almost one of premonition.

She asked as casually as she could manage, in this first moment of privacy with Kent since last night: "Did you and Miss Ashley enjoy the evening?"

"Very much. We pounded the parquet at the town's best deadfalls until the dawn drove us home with banshee screams."

Mrs. Giles's large heart filled with lead.

"I am glad, dear."

"What in heaven's name am I supposed to do?" Kent asked as he caught sight of the crowds lining the farther reaches of the avenue.

"I would just give the victory sign when they cheer, dear, and if you find me bowing to right and left stop me. This show is for you."

Suddenly, inescapably, Mrs. Giles felt terribly proud. All things, all her doubts and fears and worries, seemed so trivial, seemed to become picayune in the face of that great thing which was being done by all boys like Kent. Everything else shrank into unimportance by comparison.

A man wearing an arm band stopped Hopkins and gave him a few instructions. Just-ahead was the intersection where the official cars and the home-defense units were lined up.

It was while Hopkins had his head turned to repeat to Mrs. Giles what the man had said that the mare bolted. She reared once, plunged, and then her body lashed out with the speed of a one-heat racer.

Mrs. Giles choked back a scream. She compressed her lips and clung to the rim of the seat. She heard the explosion as a policeman gave his motorcycle the gun and shot out in front of the by now maddened mare. This only succeeded in augmenting the delirium which seemed to be attacking the animal as she careened the victoria along the avenue at sickening speed.

Kent leaped forward to climb up on the raised driver's seat to help Hopkins but was flung back. He managed to distort the fall so as to avoid crushing Mrs. Giles.

"No, no, you fool!" Mrs. Giles cried as the motorcycle policeman again swung alongside and grabbed at the near rein, while the staccato backfires of his machine completed the mare's frenzy.

The victoria, at an insane speed, crashed against the stanchion of a street lamp.

Bedlam, it seemed to Mrs. Giles, followed. The next thing she was able to grasp coherently was about an hour later. It was Mayor Saltensburg's most mellifluous and political voice.

"It is with heartfelt relief," the mayor was saying into a battery of microphones, "that I can report to you that Lieutenant Giles, by shielding his grandmother in his arms and himself bearing the full brunt of the crash, not only saved her life but enabled her to come through the accident unharmed. Michael Hopkins, the coachman, was not so fortunate. He has been taken to Central Hospital, suffering from concussion. His condition is considered serious. Lieutenant Giles, although severely shaken, is standing here beside me now. In a moment you will hear his voice."

Mrs. Giles sat very erect on the governor's right, effacing with her carriage the rips and dust of the ecru lace dress. Reaction from shock had not yet set in. She still felt numb all over, almost as though her brain were disassociated from her body. She knew that Kent, beneath his tan, was deathly pale. Dimly she was aware of Miss Ashley's face coming into focus from among the sea of faces lapping the apron of the platform. She thought Miss Ashley's expression was tragic: grim, and set, and hard, and whitened with a powdering of—was it terror? No sultry allure on it now. No, none.

Kent was talking. Mrs. Giles understood nothing of what he said. Then at length, at great length, she and Kent were being driven home by Mayor Saltensburg. They said good-by on the porch. The mayor had to dash back to see the governor off at the train.

"I think I'll go upstairs and lie down for a minute," Kent said when they were safe in the dim cool hallway.

The white, sharp agony of his face snapped Mrs. Giles right out of it. Her head cleared as though she had plunged it in ice water.

"Kent—you're suffering. You've been seriously hurt."

"Maybe something inside. Boy, am I glad that job is over."

"Can you walk upstairs?"

He could. He did. He lowered himself onto the bed. Sweat formed slowly on his skin.

"Guess it's nothing more desperate than a collarbone," he said.

Mrs. Giles went swiftly to the telephone. A miracle made it possible that Dr. Hesley could come at once. She grew a little feverish and light-headed during the twenty minutes it took him to get there. He looked at her sharply with his intelligent and kind old eyes, after she had hurried him upstairs and into Kent's room, and suggested that she wait outside the door.

The ten minutes which Mrs. Giles endured were agony. Dr. Hesley stepped out into the hall.

"He'll be all right in a few days," he said. "I've given him an injection. He wants to talk with you alone before it takes effect. I'll wait out here for you, Mrs. Giles."

She went inside and over to the bed. His hand fumbled and reached hers.

"I know you know," he said.

"Yes."

"About the other night. My getting here."

"Yes, darling."

"This thing's too big. You and I don't matter if it's what I think it is." Drugged lids were lowering. "Keep still. *Keep—still—*"

Mrs. Giles left the room and joined Dr. Hesley out in the hallway. He followed her downstairs.

"I am going to send a nurse, if I can get hold of one," he said.

"I shall stay with Kent, Doctor."

They had reached the front door, and he said to her in his friendly, heartening voice, "You are in no condition to, Mrs. Giles. I will be back after dinner. Good-by until then."

The front door closed, and for this moment by herself, alone, Mrs. Giles felt like crying from the happiness of Kent having spoken to her. She no longer felt shut out. No matter what the answer was, they were together from now on.

Leila, as usual, had come up to her on soundless feet.

"Mr. Stedman is in the drawing room," she said. "He wants to see you. He came while you were upstairs with the doctor."

"Thank you, Leila."

Mrs. Giles went in and greeted Mr. Stedman and asked him to sit down. She no longer feared him. She was filled with the strength of ten since Kent had accepted her into partnership.

"How is he?" Stedman asked.

"Dr. Hesley believes he will be all right in a few days. He has given him an injection and hopes to be able to arrange for a nurse by this evening."

"I shall only detain you for a moment." Stedman tried to plumb the curious change he felt in her expression. It was almost a glow that was making her look, yes, happy. Why in God's name should a serious accident and an invalided grandson all of a sudden make her look happy? It was beyond him. He said abruptly: "Mrs. Giles, has that horse of yours ever bolted like that before?"

"No, Mr. Stedman."

He considered this for a moment and then he said: "I am not a stupid man and you are not a stupid woman. Tell me what you have been holding back. Tell me what you know." ("Keep still," Kent's voice said to her. "*Keep still!*")

"You are mistaken, Mr. Stedman."

Stedman stood up. He walked impatiently away and then came back again. He stood looking down at her for a moment and then he shrugged.

He said. "It is you who are making the mistake, Mrs. Giles. I will do my best to convince you of that fact before it is too late. This will sound brutal to you, but I suggest you recall your view at the morgue of Russdorff's corpse."

CHAPTER 27

Stedman decided not to linger.

He considered that, having made his brutal thrust, the clever thing to do would be to leave Mrs. Giles and permit it to sink in. He wanted it to spread through her nervous system thoroughly until enough sheer fright would have accumulated to make her willing to talk.

He was not an unkind man, but he was a determined one and he honestly believed that his melodramatics would be the best thing both for Mrs. Giles and her grandson in the end. Also, he wasn't sure. He wasn't sure of anything. He was satisfied that conspiracy and murder existed and that she was involved straight up to her willowy neck. That carriage smashup not only worried him gravely, but it threw into the ash can what had been his pet theory up to date.

She was a fool. A brave, fine fool, but still one. It hurt him to watch the happiness melt from her face under the impact of that Russdorff's-corpse body blow. He wanted to relent at least a little bit and let her know that neither he nor the police were in any sense just sitting around with folded hands, but he steeled himself against doing so.

He had his own fright to contend with: the element of time. Too many balls were being juggled in the air, and his fear lay in the chance that the rhythm would be broken and the killer consequently startled into striking a second blow. He thought they were loaded with death, death of the most callous nature in the sense that it would be so impersonally bestowed. Like swatting flies.

He studied Mrs. Giles almost clinically. Had he done enough or should he loose another of the arrows in his quiver? No, this was enough. Let her taste this fright, let it keep on spreading its virus until it compelled her to talk. The sooner the better.

He said good-by. He said he would drop in and see her again after dinner. He managed to imply without in any way being rude about it that she might, by then, have come to her senses.

He had succeeded admirably, for Mrs. Giles began to suffer the first sproutings of these seeds of fear almost on the disappearance of Stedman's heels. It was a fear which was to increase with cruel gentleness through the balance of the afternoon. It would not reach its dire peak until late that night.

And all of this worry, all this filtering dread were to be with her against a background of constant concern over Kent's condition. A few moments were to stand out, and each of them in the bedlamite finish succeeded in adding its share toward building up a midnight which the Furies themselves would have found quite suitable as a haunt.

For a moment or so after Stedman's departure Mrs. Giles stayed seated in the drawing room. Although she refused to consider it, the truth was inescapable that bones and muscles did not, at seventy, have the resiliency of their younger days. In spite of Kent's wonderful shielding of her, the accident had shaken her very much. She was not unbruised, and above all else she was dog-tired.

So she sat for the next ten minutes in her armchair by a window for the plain reason that she was physically incapable of getting out of it. She heard the faint sound of the telephone ringing out in the hall and knew that Leila would answer it.

A summer shower was piling thunderheads in the sky beyond the distant hills, and it occurred to Mrs. Giles for the first time during her many years that the drawing room did have a gloomy air. Its elegance was much too ponderous and somber.

Was that detestable Miss Ashley right? And had Papa and all of his rich generation been wrong? Was this room, as Miss Ashley so concisely had put it, little better than a mausoleum suitable as a storage vault for shrouds? Heresy, yes, but wouldn't chintz—chintz, and the ponderous paintings all donated to a museum…

A change, Mrs. Giles felt, would do her good.

Leila came in and gave her a message telephoned from Central Hospital.

"Mr. Hopkins has come out of his concussion and wants to see you. The doctor wants you to come right out to the hospital because Mr. Hopkins is getting a fever from not being able to tell you something he thinks you ought to know."

Mrs. Giles compelled her aching muscles to lift her out of the chair. She went back to the kitchen and asked Ella to go up and sit in Kent's room until she returned. She consoled Ella and promised to carry her love to her husband.

When Mrs. Giles returned to the hallway Mr. Parling was coming down the stairs. Again he looked glisteningly shaved and well done in gray flannel.

He said, "Good afternoon, Mrs. Giles. I've just enjoyed the best sleep I've had since coming to Bridgehaven." He looked at his watch. "Almost time for you and your grandson to start for the reception, isn't it?"

Mrs. Giles realized that of course he wouldn't know. Daytime events would naturally be a blank to men on night shift. She told him briefly what had occurred. He was sincerely concerned.

"I have just had word that Hopkins wishes to see me. I understand it is a little urgent. You will excuse me, Mr. Parling, if I go upstairs for my things?"

"How are you going to get to the hospital?"

"I shall call a taxi."

"Let me drive you. I put the car in the stables this morning." Parling looked again at his watch. "I've plenty of time for it. You get your things on while I bring the car around to the door."

"Thank you, Mr. Parling, very much."

Mrs. Giles went upstairs. She looked in on Kent. The injection which Dr. Hesley had given him was holding him in deep sleep. She went to her rooms and put on a linen coat and hat, took gloves, and then went downstairs and out onto the porch.

Parling was waiting beside a small coupe. He helped her in and they started off.

"You'll have to tell me how to get there, Mrs. Giles."

"I will. I've just looked in on Kent."

"You're worried about him, aren't you?"

"Very worried."

"I wouldn't be. After all that he has been through in action a carriage smashup won't add up to much. The doctor would have sent him to the hospital if it were serious."

"Yes, I've thought of that. You turn left at the next crossing. Mr. Parling."

"It's something else you've got on your mind, then."

"No, I assure you."

Parling did not pursue this, and they said nothing further until he drew up before the entrance to Central Hospital. He helped her out.

"I'll park over there and then will wait for you at the reception desk."

"You are very kind."

Hopkins was in the private room which Mrs. Giles had requested the ambulance intern to give him if it happened to be vacant. It was in the wing which Papa had donated, and its windows had a pleasant view across a stretch of woodland to the river.

A nurse starched over as Mrs. Giles opened the door. She looked past the nurse to the bed where Hopkins' head, white with bandages, seemed to blend into the pillows.

"Dr. Mortlake suggests that you say as little as possible, Mrs. Giles. Just let him get whatever it is he wants to off his chest."

"Thank you, Nurse."

Mrs. Giles drew a chair close to the bed. She leaned forward and pressed one of Hopkins' old hands. The skin was cold and she could feel the bones quite plainly. I suppose, she thought, that he can feel mine too.

"We'll have you home again soon. Hopkins. Ella sends her love."

"Thank you, madam."

"Tell me what is troubling you."

"The wheel."

"Of the brougham?"

"Yes, just before we hit that lamppost. I saw the left rear wheel spinning along ahead of us. It had come off the hub."

"The jolting must have loosened it."

"It could have, but it worried me. I want you to take good care of yourself, madam."

"Thank you, Hopkins, I will."

"The wheel also made me worried about not having telephoned Mr. Stedman about where I saw Mr. Russdorff. I don't think I'm feverish about this. I think it's all linked up together. Will you tell Mr. Stedman?"

Mrs. Giles skirted the outrightness of a lie.

"I will attend to it, Hopkins."

"Now that I've placed the spot as near that tar-paper shack the scene is clearer. Mr. Russdorff wasn't alone. He was talking with some man who had his back turned toward me. I could see Mr. Russdorff's face because of the hanging electric bulb. I couldn't see the other man except for the dark outline of his back. By the time Mr. Smith and Mr. Wade came out of the shack with their luggage the man and Mr. Russdorff were gone. Perhaps Mr. Stedman can make something out of it."

"Perhaps he can."

"Then there is nothing else except my love to Ella, madam."

As she walked through the antiseptic air of the long corridor and went down in the large elevator Mrs. Giles determined on action. She asked Mr. Parling, after they were in the car, whether he would be kind enough to drop her at Merkwin's Emporium instead of taking her back to River Rest. She would take a taxi home from the store.

Parling looked toward thunderheads piling their dark hills in the western sky.

"You'll get caught, Mrs. Giles."

"I think not. My shopping will only take a minute."

"Just as you wish."

Parling observed her speculatively as he helped her out before the department store's main entrance. Shoppers were crowding from it onto the street and hurrying their steps to beat the threatening rain.

"It looks like closing time," he said. "You're just in under the wire."

CHAPTER 28

Mrs. Giles stood in the store's deep lobby, presumably fascinated with a display of three wax women having tea under a cerise-striped umbrella, until Mr. Parling's car was out of sight. She hailed with determination a taxi. She asked to be driven to the end of Joroloman Street.

The driver, who had been satisfied that he had run into all of the foibles of humanity and the quirks of life, figured that here was one he must have missed. The end of Joroloman Street was no place, in his opinion, for an old tomato of the home-James type.

"Nothing but shacks there, lady. Shacks and mud."

"So I understand."

He shrugged and clashed into high. He hustled through the modest traffic and stopped, after a ten-minute run, where the pavement came to an end. He gave her one more chance.

"This right, lady?"

"It is, thank you."

He opened the door and helped her out.

"Wait, please, driver."

"Don't worry. Can I help you across that mud?"

"No, thank you."

He stood beside the car and watched her. She seemed to know what she was doing. But nuts always did seem to. Nuts and some drunks. He'd never forget that one old turkey whom he'd driven to a house on the embankment, the way the dignified old twerp had said. "Well, good night, my man," and had stepped up to his neck straight into the river.

She was spotting that makeshift street light now. Looking down at the mud at the bottom of it. A case, all right. He watched her, fascinated, as she picked something up out of the mud. Looked like a cigarette butt. Well, for God's sake, she was putting it into her clean white kid bag. What *was* this?

Something else, now. Some torn paper which evidently had struck her mad fancy. One of these, maybe, scavenger-treasure hunts? Hadn't heard of any, not for more than a year anyhow, but with all of-these bond drives going on it was hard to keep up with the stunts.

There she dipped again. Looked like a very small bit of paper this time. Gold color, like a speck of gold confetti. Pop it went, into the bag. An apple-sized drop of rain hit him on the back of the neck.

"Hey, lady," he shouted, "she's coming down."

She nodded and was walking toward him. Unhurried. Reminded him of a lithograph his wife had of a castle in Ireland and an old dame like this one out for a breather on the lawn. Also a couple of swans.

He helped her back into the cab. She told him how to drive her home.

Mrs. Giles sat straight against the cushion and, opening the bag, examined her treasure-trove. It consisted of (the driver's eyesight had been acute) a sodden cigarette butt, the fragment of a letter, the writing of which the rain and mud had rendered completely unintelligible, and a small rectangle of paper, one side of which was glossy gold. It was very small, this last bit, scarcely wider than an eighth of an inch and not quite a quarter of an inch long. It fanned out slightly toward a torn end, something like a trellis for climbing roses.

It reminded her of something. It seemed to belong to something which, fairly recently, had caught her eye in strong sunlight. Well, it would come. She shut the bag with a snap of satisfaction.

Her clues.

The storm had increased considerably by the time they reached River Rest.

A package, Leila said as she opened the door for Mrs. Giles, had been left by a man while Mrs. Giles was out.

Mrs. Giles saw a cardboard carton over on the console table. It was untied and she lifted a flap of it. Odd—but of course: the inks. Mr. Smith had said he would attend to them. Just the suggestion of their pungent smell made her feel a brief creative urge. She took a pot out and thought it very strange. The ink wasn't black; it was green. There were other pots of course; black, brown, red, blue, yellow, and some composition that shone with the metallic glint of gold.

How very interesting.

Mrs. Giles had always confined herself to pulling prints done in the conventional sepias or black. It had never occurred to her to use color. Nor, as she recalled it, had it ever occurred to her etching instructor to do so: that kind, dyspeptic Mr. Rollo Vanderwick. It might be quite exciting. A new school.

"Take these up and leave them in the studio, please, Leila."

Leila said she would, and that there was an omelet for dinner and a good strong chicken broth for Mr. Kent when he should wake up.

Mrs. Giles went on up to Kent's room. He still slept soundly, and Ella told her that he hadn't stirred. She gave Ella the love which Hopkins had sent and asked Ella to go downstairs and send her up a tray. She would dine in Kent's room and wait there until Dr. Hesley arrived with a nurse.

It was then a quarter to six.

By half-past seven the tray which Ella had brought her was still untouched. Her eyes rarely left Kent's closed ones, and her thoughts would drift through the memories of earlier and happier moments of their lives.

Dr. Hesley came at eight. He brought with him a most competent-looking woman whom he introduced to Mrs. Giles as Nurse Jones. Mrs. Giles found herself somewhat confused and disturbed. Nurse Jones was—well, almost muscular, and offered so very little of the Florence Nightingale touch. In fact, she didn't strike Mrs. Giles as being typical of a nurse at all. A product, she supposed, of today, when nurses were as rare as almost everything else.

Dr. Hesley was satisfied with Kent's condition. He was not as satisfied, he said, with Mrs. Giles's. He thought she needed rest. A good deal of it, and certainly a sound night's sleep with breakfast in bed. He gave her some tablets and instructed her to take two of them upon retiring. She was to chase all worries from her mind, especially any regarding Kent's condition, as Nurse Jones would take care of Kent most capably.

Mrs. Giles saw that Nurse Jones was comfortably installed after Dr. Hesley had gone, then she left Kent's room and went out into the hall.

The lighting was, as it had always been, bad. Its source was a ceiling fixture made from a tortured wrought-iron pendant enclosing a globe of red glass which Papa had bought in Turkey. He had thought it very impressive. It was, all right, but it was also very sinister and ineffectual to see things by. As a little girl Mrs. Giles had always run like mad through its somber glow (it had been even worse in those days because of the gas jet which had preceded electricity) on her way to the nice bright nursery.

Perhaps it was this lighting and a subconscious reflection from her childhood fears which made Mrs. Giles think Mr. Smith's expression so strange.

Mr. Smith had been hurrying toward the stairs just as she left Kent's room and had all but knocked into her in his haste. He had his hat on and a raincoat, and possibly the shadow dropped by the hat's brim and the reddish tone which the lighting threw on his skin gave his expression that satanic cast. But there was his manner too: a distracted, almost distraught brusqueness which effaced his fine, rugged kindliness and changed it into something almost brutal. She thought he seemed possessed, if you could think of anything so demonic in a man of his stolid, forthright character.

"Watch it!" he said. "Got to go out."

And that was all, just that Mephistophelean look and the brutal rasp in his voice and he was gone: running down the stairs. The front door slammed.

The encounter increased her general nervous condition, and Mrs. Giles went on into her rooms in a state. She put the envelope which Dr. Hesley had given her on the bed table. She had no intention of taking them, although the temptation to do so was very strong. What heaven it would be: a good night's rest.

But the gloom of rain on the windowpanes and the seeds of fear which Mr. Stedman had so pointedly sown were filling her with the most uncomfortable premonitions about the night. A voice within her warned her strongly against drugged sleep. Be up, the voice told her, and be on guard. She had learned during the many years of her life to pay attention to such voices.

Nurse Jones disturbed her. It was not the time when doctors could be given a choice, could send for a nurse who they knew from experience would be reliable. Was Nurse Jones a nurse at all?

Where *was* it she had seen something similar to that fleck of gold-faced paper which she had retrieved from the mud near that shack? In full sunlight she had seen its counterpart and then, yes, she had seen it once again in partial shadow.

And what had happened to kind and sturdy Mr. Smith? What news, what shock could have come to him to have produced that menacing tornado effect out in the hall? Had his handsome young nephew been affected too?

Then Leila came in and said that Mr. Stedman would be happy if Mrs. Giles would be kind enough to join him for a moment down in the drawing room.

CHAPTER 29

Mrs. Giles took a moment to refresh her toilet. This coming encounter with Mr. Stedman would be, she felt, the moment for the drawing of the net. She wanted the buttress of looking her best. Her cheeks were terribly gray, and she decided that a slight rouging would do them no harm. She also touched up the bloodless look of her lips.

A grandfather clock struck nine as she walked slowly down the stairs. The chimes were Westminster and some of the notes were off key, but they floated with dignity up past her ears and spread through the cloud of brooding which seemed clamped upon the house. She wondered whether Miss Ashley were back from the plant. There had been no sound of Miss Ashley about, or any *feel* of her.

Mr. Stedman was standing squarely before the drawing room's hearth, now graced with its summer decor of a fan-shaped arrangement of decorative grasses. Mrs. Giles took a good look at his rooted imperturbability as she advanced into the room and decided that he was there to stay. Certainly his stance said he had no intention of budging until he got what he had come for. She drew together the tattered remnants of her bodily strength and asked him to sit down.

He declined. He remained standing. He waited until she was seated in an armchair and then he said: "Mrs. Giles, I am going to ask you to be frank."

She looked for a longer moment at him, and he seemed filled with knowledge, stuffed with a full awareness of all of the things which she had tried so miserably to withhold from him. It would be difficult to fence.

"I am completely at your disposal, Mr. Stedman."

"No, it is evasions such as that one which I hope we can avoid. We both know you are not. You are bound by a quixotic and stupid desire to protect your grandson. Will it help you if I assure you he needs no protection of the nature you are offering him? Neither the police nor I are such stereotyped fools as to believe that Lieutenant Giles, after a year of battle service in the South Pacific, flew to Washington and then on to Bridgehaven and spent the first hour of his arrival in cold-bloodedly murdering an international crook."

It was very tempting.

"Naturally," Mrs. Giles said quietly, "anything of that nature would be impossible for a man of Kent's character. You will permit me to correct you? He reached here yesterday morning—that is, the morning pursuant to Mr. Russdorff's murder—by train."

Stedman walked over to a side table and opened a brief case. He took out two photographic enlargements. He handed one to Mrs. Giles and said: "Take a look at that, please. It is a very small segment of the news picture which was taken of you by the cameraman of the Bridgehaven *Gazette* while you were standing on the station platform. This was shortly after Lieutenant Giles had left the train. It is greatly enlarged."

Mrs. Giles remembered only too well. Slowly from her feet and from her finger tips ice crept inward through her veins and approached her heart. She could even recall the cameraman's brash remark as the flash bulb flicked and he shouted at her: "*That's* the stuff we want, sister."

Well, there she was, at least that small segment of her which the enlargement had encompassed: her eyes, her hand with the handkerchief crumpled in its fingers, and escaping from the handkerchief which was busied with wiping away her tears hung Kent's identification tag and a section of the bracelet's chain.

It was no use.

"Well, Mr. Stedman?"

"My secretary noticed this and brought it to my attention. In common with every other young woman in town, she is romantically flat on her face about your grandson. She had not been able to take in the reception at the station, so her interest in the newspaper account, especially those press shots of Lieutenant Giles, were gone over with a magnifying glass. The pictures, literally so. The touch about his having had his identification tag torn from his wrist and about it later having been found on the platform and restored to him was included in the general report. Well, she thought it odd—that recognizable metal tag dangling from the handkerchief in your hand."

"Yes, Mr. Stedman."

"Oh, for heaven's sake, Mrs. Giles, don't take this so tragically. The story was perfectly simple to reconstruct. Here, look at this other enlargement. You will see it shows the imprint of a woman's bedroom slipper in the moist earth close to Russdorff's body. Even sheer dolts would have examined the various slippers in this house. The police went through every room while all of you were down at the morgue."

(At least, Mrs. Giles thought swiftly, the search had taken place after she had basted the blue silk wrapper inside the dinner dress. But if the slippers had been found was the wrapper of any consequence? Better attack.)

"You found that a pair of mine were damp," she said.

The admission pleased Stedman. Evidently she was softening up.

"Yes. Naturally at that moment it was too soon to know just where we stood. We knew that during the night or early morning you had observed the body and, for some reason which must have been an urgent one, had decided not to inform the police. We were considerably puzzled as to why a woman of your character and standing would do a thing like that."

Stedman took a turn, as though debating how far to go. He said, "We had no knowledge then that Lieutenant Giles had reached Bridgehaven hours before he was expected. We still thought of him as being on a train en route here from Washington. Is it any wonder that we were forced to consider that you had murdered the man yourself?"

"None. I can easily understand it."

"Take that bit of blue silk from your wrapper."

(So this too. All of her cleverness a futile waste.)

"You knew that the wrapper was mine?"

"We knew, Mrs. Giles, that you owned a blue silk wrapper. That astonishing maid of yours told the police so before they searched for the damp slippers. Naturally they were unable to locate it. Where did you hide it up to the time when you buried it beneath the delphiniums this morning?"

"Did the man on patrol duty see me, Mr. Stedman?"

"The light being turned on in your bedroom at four in the morning of course interested him. The flashlight flickering in the tool shed. His instructions were simply to observe. Where did you keep the wrapper hidden, Mrs. Giles?"

"I basted it inside a dinner dress and left it hanging in the wardrobe."

He observed her with the respect he usually reserved for an accomplished crook. How pitiful the rouge looked against the white of her cheeks.

She said quietly, "Is this a prelude to my arrest, Mr. Stedman?"

"I have already asked you not to consider this so tragically, Mrs. Giles. I am not a wolf who is here to eat you. It is true that we more than ever considered you as our best bet after we had learned Russdorff's identity. Because of his record, which, as I told you, largely included blackmail."

Mrs. Giles was sincerely bewildered.

"How on earth could he blackmail me?"

Stedman smiled.

"We did not know. We did know that you were a very rich woman and that your life has in recent years been a fairly lonely one. Certainly so far as publicity is concerned you have been anything but an open book."

"I am naturally retiring, Mr. Stedman."

"Yes, we knew we were wrong and crossed you off as a suspect right after the identification-tag business. Lieutenant Giles hadn't had it torn from him by the welcoming mob. You yourself had dropped it onto the platform. Why? So it would be found there. Why? So that it wouldn't be found where it had originally fallen. The inference was elemental. You had found the tag by Russdorff's body and you had not called the police because of your desire to shield Lieutenant Giles."

"As you say, Mr. Stedman, those things are entirely inferential."

"Not really. We checked back then, you see. We established your grandson's arrival from Washington by plane at ten o'clock that night. We established his backtracking along the line after the crime had been committed and his waiting in a station until morning so that he could reach Bridgehaven on the proper train. Those things are very simple."

"I see now that they are."

"The crime itself is not simple. Neither the motive for it nor the killer. We continue puzzled. Badly so. The knife that killed Russdorff has proven valueless as a clue to its owner. There are no fingerprints on its hilt. With the exception of the one made by your bedroom slipper, all footprints in the vicinity are useless. There seemed a thousand of them, left by the rush of people who came here that morning to rent rooms."

Had he lulled her now enough? Had he convinced her sufficiently of the high altruism of his intent? He hesitated a briefest instant and then said, "Mrs. Giles, that night was a very silent one. The storm had stopped. What time was it when you heard Russdorff cry out as he was struck?"

"There was no cry. Just that scuffling sound down on the gravel."

Stedman expelled a deep breath of relief. He grimaced.

"I hate to trick things out of you like that. There seemed no other way."

He sat down. He looked at her with kindness. He held no doubt whatever but that she was in her grandson's confidence and could inform him of the essential lead. Surely the bulk of these generous loaves which he had cast upon the waters would come back home.

It had been worth it. Both the effort and all of his patience during the past two days. At last she would talk. Swiftly, then, they could reach within the murk of this mess and catch their man.

"Tell me now," he said. "Start with the scuffle. Tell me everything from there."

The ice had reached her heart by now, and her whole body lacked comfort and warmth, and she thought that if she once started to tremble an ague would grip her and she would never be able to stop. It was so difficult to think when you felt sick like this, sick all through with doubts and worry and indecision.

How greatly if at all did this assurance of knowledge on Mr. Stedman's part release her from Kent's injunction that she keep still? Kent's voice, so earnest, so saturated with the imminence of a threat which was imperiling this nation which he loved so much, which both of them loved so much: how *could* she betray him further than (because of Mr. Stedman's trickery) she already had?

"My grandson is sleeping under the influence of an injection given him by Dr. Hesley."

"I know that, Mrs. Giles."

"You have told me that you trust him. I shall ask you to keep that trust, Mr. Stedman, until Kent wakes."

She was slipping from him again. Like an eel, Stedman thought, no matter how aristocratic a one. Secretly he admired this stubborn streak even as it annoyed him. He had few notes left to play with which to seduce her, to break her down. He was thoroughly frustrated and cold with anger, although this was the last thing which his manner showed. He took a fresh grip. His air of kindliness increased.

"The smashup of the brougham, the reception at City Hall, your grandson's collapse right after it, all of those things prevented me from questioning him at once upon our conclusions concerning the identification tag. I am still prevented. It will be morning before Lieutenant Giles shakes off the effect of the injection. Dr. Hesley has told me so. There is the night."

"Night?"

"Certainly. There are hours of it left. Hours during which we remain blindfolded until he talks. Russdorff's murder was no common crime. Our brief belief that your grandson was his killer, whether from self-defense or whatever, was cancelled by the incident of the brougham when his own life was purposely put in jeopardy."

"Purposely, Mr. Stedman?"

"Did you think we would ignore that sudden madness of the mare? Fail to have her examined by a veterinarian? We know that American hemp did the trick, had probably been mixed in with her feed. Well, that didn't work. And do you think this murderous train will stop? Now?"

She was frightened sick.

"Kent is my grandson. I love him, Mr. Stedman, more than anything on earth. But he is a soldier too."

Stedman drew a handkerchief from his pocket and wiped light sweat from his brow. She had beaten him. Thrown that final stubborn negation straight in his face, wrapped up in a background of the national anthem. When you came right down to it, what sound reason was there for any such grandiloquent implications? Simply because Russdorff was a polyglot fusion of God knew how many nationalities and was listed on the records as an international crook.

And also because if you looked at it otherwise it made so little sense. People went a little mad these days. It took but the smallest pressure to distort the commonplace. He wondered whether he himself might not be suffering from this common complaint. It could have been a meeting of pure chance, and young Giles might have resented some crack which Russdorff made. As elemental as that. No, it couldn't have. It wasn't that kind of homicide. There was the knife. That above everything else, in Stedman's opinion, let out young Giles.

He stood up and replaced the enlargements in the brief case. He zipped it closed.

He said, "The patrol has moved into the grounds itself. The patrolman will hear you, Mrs. Giles, should you find it necessary to call out."

CHAPTER 30

The house was empty.

It wasn't, of course, and Mrs. Giles knew it, but that was the impression it gave her. Mr. Smith was out, expending his curious restrained fury on whatever its objective may have been, and Miss Ashley was out so far as Mrs. Giles knew.

But Kent was asleep upstairs in his room under the eye of that disturbingly muscular Nurse Jones, and young Mr. Wade could be in, while Leila and Ella were definitely in the kitchen. Still, she felt alone.

She sat there in this immutable emptiness, summing up the deadly high lights of the past two days in an effort to arrive at some coherence out of their confusions. The high lights were significant but few, and while she brooded on them the minutes, like a long and lethargic fuse, crept ticking toward the powder keg of midnight.

They centered on Kent.

Mrs. Giles abjured coincidence or chance. Purpose had altered Kent's planned departure from Washington and had sent him on ahead of time by plane. She supposed he would have had small difficulty in getting one, not only from his present prominence in the force but also through his wide acquaintanceship with other fliers in the service.

Then the fate lines of three people met at a common point: Kent, Miss Ashley, and Mr. Russdorff, with the common point being the gravel driveway below her sitting-room window. Had this triple joining been purposed too? Death made Mrs. Giles think it had not. Kent and Miss Ashley, yes: the whole atmosphere of that rendezvous had reeked of the prearranged. Then Mr. Russdorff's entry upon it had been the unexpected, the unplanned note. And Mr. Russdorff died.

Then, the lie. The acted lie so poorly done by Kent, and so professionally accomplished by Miss Ashley, of never having met prior to that public introduction at the morgue. Or had Miss Ashley's professional performance been marred by those two touches of the false forwarding address and the contradictory statements as to the plant in which she worked as a gun inspector?

What was the story she had fabricated to send Kent off from the murdered Mr. Russdorff and into furtive flight? Surely it had plucked loudly upon the strings of patriotism in some form. Nothing else would have shackled him to such willing collaboration.

How closely, Mrs. Giles wondered, did the things which she knew combine with those of Mr. Stedman's theories, theories which had struck Mrs. Giles as very vague ones. As much so in fact as were her own.

What of Mr. Stedman's feeling that murder had been aimed at Kent? The brougham smashup pointed vividly toward that end. But one thing, and probably the most important thing of all, Mr. Stedman did not know: Miss Ashley's connection with the situation. The scarlet thread of her ran through it all like thin bright danger.

Yes, Miss Ashley.

It boiled down to that.

Westminster chimes announced the half-hour. That would be half-past ten. Mrs. Giles stood up. She felt she had decided nothing, and still the pressure to grasp some decision had grown into urgent necessity. She would go upstairs and see whether Miss Ashley was in, and if she was Mrs. Giles intended to drag from her the truth.

Miss Ashley was not in her room, and the room held that completely undisturbed look which convinced Mrs. Giles that Miss Ashley had not entered it since Leila had tidied it in the morning. She was satisfied that Miss Ashley had not returned that evening from the plant.

Once more out in the hall and walking through the depressing glow of its dull red lighting, Mrs. Giles was aware, as she passed his door, that young Mr. Wade was home. There were sounds coming from behind the door, almost, she thought for a puzzled moment, as though a heavy piece of furniture were being moved.

She went in to see Kent. Nurse Jones was sitting implacably muscular in a chair near a window. A shaded night light shone on a magazine in her hand. So far as Mrs. Giles could make out, its title was *True*-something.

"Is he all right?"

"Perfectly, Mrs. Giles. I suggest that you follow Dr. Hesley's advice and go to bed."

"You would call me, of course?"

"Certainly. Don't forget the sedative tablets you are to take. Good night, Mrs. Giles."

"Good night, Nurse."

Mrs. Giles went to her rooms. She carried the look of Kent's face on his pillow with her. The peaceful helplessness of it: so open, through the betrayal of drugged sleep, to undefended attack.

Mr. Stedman's alarms over Kent's safety persistently beset her. What *could* occur? How *could* the feet of murder step past the patrol on the grounds and, once inside the house, step softly up, then, quelling the gorgon Nurse Jones, step onward into within reach of Kent?

Mrs. Giles frankly did not know. But she was taking no chances. She went to her desk and took a revolver of .44 caliber from a hidden compartment. The gun had been one of Papa's which he had bought from a sheriff while touring Texas in the old Stanley Steamer. It had a pearl handle, and Papa regretted the fact later. He always felt he should have gotten the sort with notches in it in case he ever had to add one.

Now that the gun was in her hand Mrs. Giles wondered what to do with it. It seemed so sizable. She called upon her fund of literary precedents. She tried it in several handbags, but its outline was as noticeable as though it were openly carried in full sight. A muff was of course absurd. She recalled one extremely early opus in which a garter had been employed most effectively, but apart from the fact that garters were no longer in existence Papa's gun was far too heavy for anything like that.

She rummaged in a bureau drawer of odds and ends, and a large knitting bag which Elsa Marfoot had given her last Christmas seemed the perfect solution. Mrs. Giles, who did not knit, had never used it. As she had no yarns, she stuffed a sweater into the bag and bedded the gun in its folds.

Then she went downstairs to wait.

CHAPTER 31

Fergus added the last pair of serviceable socks to his stuffed suitcase. They were drab affairs in workmanlike gray and diametrically different from the gaudy raiment in which it was his usual pleasure to indulge. They were symbolic to his backward mind of this whole unpleasant venture.

His deepest displeasure lay in the fact that his role had called upon him, at the shop, to work. And there had been the endless delays. His basic nature (a physician had once given him a working-over and had mentioned glands) was all animal and, as such, amoral almost to a complete degree.

He was burning into a slow temper which was laced with fear. Smith's own rage had touched on panic just before Smith had lunged out into the night, and the panic had communicated itself to Fergus. To his feral brain it had turned River Rest into a jungle with himself deserted, no matter how momentarily, and at bay.

He felt on his own, beset through a thoroughly mysterious quirk of chance with secret dangers. His first thought had embraced nothing but a primal urge to escape from what his simple reasoning could identify as nothing less than a menacing trap.

But escape to what? He was completely penniless, for he spent money as soon as it reached his pocket, and in this disgusting world at war, where men of his age and physique were open at any moment of the day to official questioning, where would he be without Smith?

If he had money he would be all right without Smith. That thought had come while he was throwing his shirts into the bag. Suppose, he wondered, the thing were still in the house? A blaze of hope shot through the jungle. If he could but lay his hands on it and *then* skip, escape would be assured.

He could sell out to the others.

He wondered feverishly how much he could get. Thousands and thousands of dollars surely. With such a fortune as a stake he could hit Mexico, the coast of which he knew reasonably well from calls at Tampico, Port Lobos, and varying ports while working on a tanker.

The prospect dazzled. He shut the suitcase and snapped its hasps and lock. He went into the bathroom and looked at his face in the mirror. Better cool it off with cold water, he decided. Better do a job on his hair.

Before he looked the old woman up.

CHAPTER 32

At eleven o'clock Mrs. Giles left the drawing room and went back into the kitchen. She sent Ella and Leila up to bed. She told them that she herself would attend to the lights and to locking up. She refused a suggested sandwich and a glass of milk.

As she returned along the hall she caught sight of the flash of a match being struck outside in the vestibule. She saw its gleam through the stained-glass panel of various geometrical figures which Papa had had put into the door.

Mrs. Giles stood still in the hall's amber light for perhaps a minute. Mr. Stedman was the first thought that came to her, but the bell did not ring. The curiously harried Mr. Smith? He had a key and yet the door did not open.

Queer, she thought.

Looking anything but willowy, Mrs. Giles took a firm and utterly impractical clutch on the knitting bag. Her six-shooter technique, although all right in theory, was almost suicidal in practice. She opened the front door herself.

A startled, burly man in a policeman's raincoat spun around and faced her. He took the cigarette he had just lighted from his lips.

"Catching a drag or two out of the rain," he said. "You're Mrs. Giles?"

"Yes, officer."

"I'm the patrol. Last night I was mostly out on the main road, but tonight they've moved me into the grounds." He looked glumly out at the depressing downpour. "It's a rotten night."

"Would you care to wait inside?"

"Thank you, I couldn't do that. I shouldn't even be up here in the vestibule, but I've been traipsing in this flood since eight."

"I wonder whether you noticed one of my guests, a Miss Ashley, either coming in or going out this evening?"

"Would she be the one who went off in a taxi last night with Lieutenant Giles? Her looking all like an angel in white?"

Mrs. Giles repressed an antonym of "angelic."

"Yes."

"I recall her well. I recall her from the fact of their dismissing the cab before it was even out of my sight and their walking straight back here and through the gates."

"They—they returned directly to the house? Right after they had left?"

"Whether the house or not I could not say, but into the grounds they went, and not another sight of them. I thought it a pity. Such a fine pair, the two of them."

"A pity, officer?"

"What else could it have been but a spat? I am hoping it's healed by now. That's me, Mrs. Giles. Beatrice, my wife, says I'm little more than a great big bag of romance."

Mrs. Giles preferred more concrete information and less of the love-lorn-column ilk. She was fully determined to back that asp-like hussy up against a figurative wall and have it out.

"Then you *did* see Miss Ashley tonight?"

"No ma'am. Not tonight. The only ones tonight since I've been on were the doctor and a stocky gentleman breathing fire and Mr. Stedman. They all came out of the house. Nobody yet has gone in."

The fire-breathing specimen would naturally have been poor, excited Mr. Smith.

"Thank you, officer."

"You are welcome, ma'am."

Mrs. Giles returned to her chair in the drawing room. It was placed near the entrance at a vantage point which gave her a clear view of the front door. This later information bewildered her completely: the fact that Kent and Miss Ashley had dismissed the taxicab and walked back at once into the grounds.

They had gone to no hot spots, an obvious fact both from Miss Davis' having been unable to locate them and from the policeman's statement, even though Kent had considered it expedient in the victoria to prevaricate about it. No, they had come back to River Rest.

And then?

Had they entered while she had been upstairs in the studio with Mr. Smith and Mr. Wade? Or sooner even, while they had all been here in the drawing room? Again the irritating veils of deception baffled her. The silence which had marked their presence. The concealment which they must have effected during the nightly tour of Leila turning the lights out and locking up.

Was that woman in the house right *now*? Brewing her witch's broth for Kent's deeper ensnarement? Perverting his mind to her own evil uses under the star-sprinkled banner of patriotism? Invisible and yet here?

Her aptitude for astrology hinted at the occult. How right she had been about the year 1928 and, yes, how equally so in her warning of not to travel. If you could call a ride in a victoria travel. But why not? Surely the essence of strange foresight had been there.

Was Mr. Stedman wrong? Had the victoria attempt at murder been directed not against Kent but against Hopkins, with herself just thrown in as excess ballast? The original plan had been for Kent to ride in the official car with Mayor Saltensburg and not in the victoria. Yes, sense preferably pointed to Hopkins as the target.

To kill Hopkins before he remembered where it was he had seen Mr. Russdorff?

Before he recalled the man whom Russdorff had been talking to: the man of whom Hopkins had viewed nothing but a back? The man (could this be true?) *who was to become Mr. Russdorff's murderer?* Who well could have feared that Hopkins had viewed more than just a back?

A sodden cigarette butt—a torn section of an illegible letter—a fleck of gold-faced paper which once in sunlight and once in partial shadow… Mrs. Giles's tired old head started to nod.

A sound jerked it upright.

Fergus Wade was standing in the doorway.

The grandfather clock struck twelve.

CHAPTER 33

Fergus had done a good job.

His temper was once more completely under leash and a low, clever cunning smoothly in its place. The house was still a jungle, but he himself was no longer at bay. Rather, he felt supreme, a king of beasts, stalking on sure and softly padded feet his prey.

This weak old woman.

How simple the setup seemed. The servants were all in their roosts in bed. And even if they hadn't been, what of it? One fragile zany and two wraiths. The grandson was knocked out of the picture with a shot of dope. The nurse was anchored by his bedside. Suppose she did start moving? She was nothing but another woman.

Fergus smiled shyly and walked into the drawing room.

"I didn't mean to disturb you. The house was so quiet, I thought everyone was asleep. I'm worried about my uncle."

Relief flooded Mrs. Giles. How clean and fresh and workmanlike he looked: a breath of clear air through the miasma of her nightmarish thoughts.

"I saw your uncle when he left, Mr. Wade. He struck me, too, as being perturbed."

"It's gone, you see."

Mrs. Giles didn't.

"Something of your uncle's?"

"Yes. That etching of yours which he bought at the bond sale." Fergus' eyes bathed her with candor. "Uncle was very fond of it, Mrs. Giles."

"But I don't understand."

"Well, he didn't notice it right away. The rain got us pretty wet coming back from the shop, and he took a bath and changed his clothes and then he noticed that the etching wasn't on the wall. Uncle's awfully funny sometimes. Little things will send him into a fury."

Light was beginning to break, at least in so far as to where the etching probably was. Its newness in Mr. Smith's room had undoubtedly caught Leila's attention while she had been tidying up, and the etching had simply appealed to her kleptomaniac fancy. What a pity poor Mr. Smith had worked himself into such a stew.

"I got thinking about it after Uncle was gone," Fergus was saying. "I don't know much about artists. But I thought that maybe you had taken it, Mrs. Giles. To sign your name to it or something, like they do in books."

Mrs. Giles got up from the chair.

"No, not that, Mr. Wade, but I am reasonably certain I can find it for your uncle."

He looked at her with charming diffidence while a curious flush spread slowly upward over his face.

"That would be very lucky, Mrs. Giles."

She was averse to telling him outright her strong assurance that Leila had taken it. The less that Leila were brought to the attention of this ruggedly bashful Adonis, the better. Also, it seemed so unkind to spread the nature of Leila's unfortunate habit. What a marvelous color young Mr. Wade had. Wind-swept.

"Where is it?" he asked quietly.

"I will see that it is replaced on the wall in the morning."

What a quick reflex in the muscles of his fingers!

"I'd be grateful if you could get it for me now, Mrs. Giles. I'd like Uncle to find it there when he comes back."

"Come with me, Mr. Wade."

Mrs. Giles hooked the knitting bag over an arm and led the way upstairs. She wondered as he followed her on quiet feet through the ruby-tinted hall what reason she could offer for the etching being now in Leila's cache. She hesitated for an instant before Kent's door but then repressed a natural impulse to look in. How softly young Mr. Wade walked. She would scarcely know that he was following her.

So softly, and still as they mounted the stairs to the attic floor his breathing was becoming audible, even though the silence lingered in his feet. Curious that Mr. Smith should have made such a to-do. Surely he must have known she would gladly have given him another India print of the placid stag at eventide at peace beside the forest pool.

She pressed a switch, and the studio sprang into light. Fergus followed her inside and closed the door.

"Is it in here, Mrs. Giles?"

"Yes."

"Why? Who brought it here? Did you?"

The voice had taken on a lower, a vibrant note, and for the first moment since she had been enchanted by it Mrs. Giles had the disturbing impression that Mr. Wade's bashful smile was not quite *nice*. It seemed unchanged, but there was a faint distortion about it, and a smoky look had come into his eyes.

She found herself fascinated just watching them while the large bright room receded blurringly and only his eyes were alive with embers slowly hinted. Avarice, a triumphant greed, like that look which Papa had described on the face of a friend of his who had been prospecting for years and had at last struck gold.

"Get it." The voice wasn't a whisper. It was too choked, but its effect was of a whisper. "Get it, Mrs. Giles."

She found herself saying, "Why?"

"I've told you why."

"Are you well, Mr. Wade?"

"I said to get it, Mrs. Giles."

He walked softly toward her, step by gentle step.

(What *could* occur? How *could* the feet of murder step past the patrol on the grounds and, once inside the house, step softly up, then, quelling the gorgon Nurse Jones, step onward into within reach of Kent?)

"What have you done to him? What have you done to my grandson?"

"Get me that etching quick before Smith gets back."

She had the gun half out of the knitting bag when it caught in a fold of the sweater. He took it gently from her, bag and all, and slung it into a corner of the room. He took her wrist in his fingers, and for an instant she knew blind pain.

"I wouldn't do that, Fergus," Mr. Smith's voice said from the door-way.

Pain eased and her eyes cleared, and Mrs. Giles brought Mr. Smith into focus. He took a chair and brought it to her.

"Sit down, Mrs. Giles. I saw that the studio windows were lighted. I found my nephew's bags packed. It seemed advisable to come up."

Absurdly she wanted to cry. She felt that her brain had snapped. Death had brushed her because of the little stag. No, surely not. Some-thing of vastly greater worth. Something that had been placed within the casement of the etching's frame? Which had ripped to shreds her sound estimation of these two men's fineness and exposed them in the color of blood?

And Kent?

"How much has he told you?" Smith asked her.

"Nothing."

"What did you tell her, Fergus?"

"You heard her."

Smith drew his breath in deeply, then he sighed.

"It doesn't matter now. This setup is ended. I should have known it was too perfect. Get the etching, Mrs. Giles."

"Is the etching why Mr. Russdorff was killed?"

He said indifferently, "Yes."

She managed to stand up. She lingered for a moment's regret over the solidity with which Papa had built the house. This room which he had converted for her use into a studio had been the children's playroom. Neither the happy shrieks of games nor running feet had sifted out of it to disturb the quiet below.

"I shall not give it to you, Mr. Smith."

He said with frank curiosity, "Why?"

Deep inside herself she knew the answer without, in a sense, knowing it all. Kent and Miss Ashley and Mr. Russdorff and the scuffle on the gravel drive. Mr. Russdorff had been murdered because of her etching or for what its frame contained. The roached dark mare had bolted into murderous flight. And Kent had said to her: "You and I don't matter if it's what I think it is." So even Kent himself was not quite sure. But he had been sure enough to risk an awful lot. And Mr. Smith wanted it now.

He was quietly talking again.

"You are an intuitive woman, Mrs. Giles, and, I am sure, a brave one. You have common sense. We will take the etching, and then Fergus and I will be gone. You will return to the gracious life you have always known. I will tell you this about Fergus. He does not kill. His value to us, to myself and to my associates, lies in other fields. He is an expert at persuasion. He is an artist at it. You see, he has no nerves."

A moment drew to its close.

"I'm afraid you'll have to, Fergus, after all," Smith said. Smith did not care to watch. He turned his back and faced the door he had just closed. But it was not closed. The man standing on the threshold was a stranger. Obviously he had just come in from the rain. His overcoat was wet, and a drop or two were falling from the brim of his dark felt hat. He held a revolver in his hand in a manner which informed Smith that the man was familiar with guns. A silencer bloated the revolver's end.

"Have they hurt you, Mrs. Giles?" Parling said.

CHAPTER 34

So profoundly glad was she to see him that Mrs. Giles was incapable of considering the coincidental patness of Mr. Parling's appearance on the scene, or of delving into the magic which had caused a man, supposedly miles away from the house on a night shift, to show up in the nick of time.

In the state her mind was in (which was no state at all) Mr. Parling's role of *deus ex machina* was no stranger to her than the old pantomimes for which, in Mrs. Giles's childhood, Mamma had arranged box parties at Christmastide for her and her school friends. Always, in the pantomimes, the forces of evil were routed by the good fairy and vanished to a satisfactory stewing through the trap doors out of which they had so recently popped.

Not that there was anything fey about Mr. Parling right then. She did wish he hadn't struck Mr. Smith and Mr. Wade quite so hard with that short leather thing with a knob on it. They looked almost dead: slumped like two straw men at the base of Payne and Sons' Albion hand press, where they had fallen. Evil though they were, certainly they were now fangless, and she worried about them.

"Shouldn't Dr. Hesley be called, Mr. Parling? Or at least Nurse Jones?"

Sheer disbelief and fondness played fractionally in Failing's eyes.

"You just sit quietly, Mrs. Giles. Get your wind back. Then you can give me the plates and we'll go downstairs and phone Stedman."

"Plates?"

"Yes. Didn't you get it? From anything they said?"

"I'm afraid—I am sorry, but my head is so very confused."

He almost smiled.

"You know, Mrs. Giles, you will think this odd. I wondered about *you*. Whether you were mixed up in it. So many families such as yours have lost their money. You might have been tempted. You had the printing press and the supplies of paper. Your position and the reputation of this house made such a perfect front."

"This is all completely unintelligible, Mr. Parling. I think if you would be simple about it…?"

She listened earnestly while he talked. Her head cleared somewhat, and it did begin to make sense. These coincidental appearances, the bravura of these nicks-of-time were nothing extraordinary when you considered the canvas as a whole. There was nothing "coincidental" in organized crime, he told her. Or in its prosecution. The stakes were too high on both sides to permit of it. He led her lucidly through intricacies.

Smith was one of the finest forgers of government bank notes in the country. Perhaps the very finest. They had tried to get on his trail for a long time but had never until recently been able to, and his fingerprints were not on record. Wade had never been caught up with either; he, too, was not on record, a fact which, in addition to his other abilities, made him highly serviceable to Smith and the rest of the mob.

They had been able, because of this recordless slate, to obtain jobs in a war plant. Their credentials, of course, had been forged by Smith, to whom such trifles would be child's play. As war workers they had felt their fronts to be secure, not only from the draft but from chance suspicion by the law. These were not the days when idle men went long unobserved.

(Why don't you, Mrs. Giles thought irrelevantly, put the bracelets on them? Wasn't that always done? It did seem a bit extreme to knock them out so coldly when a kinder tap and handcuffs would, it appeared to her, have done the trick.)

The job which Smith and his mob was now engaged on was not a simple one in the sense of being an ordinary attempt to print and shove the queer. It impinged on the war. Did Mrs. Giles know that the paper money paid to our troops in Africa differed from money here in that the seal of the United States was printed in gold? She did not. This was done, Parling said, to prevent the Axis from circulating United States currency seized from banks in Europe.

(Mrs. Giles's aching head was off again. Gold. Again the color tantalized her: that fleck of gold-faced paper which in sunshine and in shadow... How soothing Mr. Parling's voice was. So sane. Like water cool on fever.)

She would easily understand. Parling went on, the inestimable value to Axis agents of a first-class forgery job of such currency. A truly first-class one which attained perfection, one such as perhaps Smith alone could turn out.

Getting the forged bills over there offered nothing insurmountable. Possibly Mrs. Giles had read that recent newspaper report where a plan to have gold bullion minted here into coins and then to transport them abroad by submarine had been scotched? Well, there had been such a plan, and this one which Smith's mob had embarked on was completely similar.

(Dear Kent! So this was it. So this was *why*. That dreadful money poured among the natives, weaning away their allegiance to the Allied cause, then the useless, cruel, wasted deaths piled onto the sum of our men.)

But in the carefullest chain of planning, Parling said, there were imponderables which could express themselves in a weakening link. The human equation never in history had been sound. In this case, Russdorff. His international connections had bestowed on him the role of middleman between the Axis and Smith's mob.

Naturally he was greedy. Such men always are. The limitations of their honor were the bonds of cash. Their lives were milestoned with forty pieces of silver. Their coat of arms, the double cross. This deal of Smith's mob was not unknown.

Mrs. Giles would not be aware of it, but such items of news had a habit of running through the underworld like a secret river. (Parling was wrong in this. Mrs. Giles was excellently aware of the fact.) A rival mob to Smith's was determined to highjack the job if it could. And this simply meant stealing Smith's plates. They were the core, the very heart, of all forgery: the plates. Whoever had them had all. Even the government was checkmated on a forgery case until the actual plates were in its agent's possession.

Naturally Russdorff was delighted. Instead of just skimming off the undoubtedly handsome commission arranged for with Smith's mob he would manage to steal the plates and hand them over to the proposed highjackers for a far handsomer sum.

"You will wonder," Parling told Mrs. Giles, "why he failed." They must have met, Russdorff and the leader of the rival mob, several times. Undoubtedly there had been such a meeting on the night when Russdorff was killed. What had occurred? You could imagine, if you were familiar with the way of such things. Russdorff certainly did not have, as yet, the plates. For Smith had those so cleverly concealed, as the recent scene had proved, in the framing of Mrs. Giles's little etching.

Perhaps the leader of the rival mob did, on the other hand, have the money to turn over for delivery? Perhaps from Russdorff's actions he grew suspicious that the double cross would bloom into a triple one? Perhaps he feared that Russdorff, after this unsatisfactory meeting, would run at once and tell Smith of this rival mobster's plans? Naturally, for a price. Nothing with the Russdorffs of this world came free.

(Was something wrong here? Mrs. Giles wondered. Was this quite *right*? It seemed so very sensible. So plain. The fatal dicker would have been the one which Hopkins had seen from the box of the brougham between Mr. Russdorff and that man who had exposed nothing but his back to Hopkins' view. That man whom Mrs. Giles now understood plainly to have been the leading mobster of the highjack gang.)

With all that in mind, Parling said, the rest must surely be plain. The rival leader had followed Russdorff and had been satisfied when he saw him enter the gates of River Rest that the triple cross was definitely on the make. So he had stabbed Russdorff and made off, to cook up some other scheme for getting hold of the plates. Russdorff would have to be dead. Otherwise he would have exposed the rival gangster's identity to Smith.

So much, Parling said, he had been able to determine. As to who this rival mobster was, frankly he didn't know. And, now that the plates were safe, he did not care. Tonight's imbroglio was as simple as it had been unimportant. The etching had left Smiths' wall and come up here. Mrs. Giles evidently knew the answer to that one.

Smith, in a fever of fear and rage, had rushed out of the house to contact the new agent who had taken Russdorff's place. Parling knew this was so because he had followed Smith to his destination and then had followed him back here to the house. Wade, alone, had in some fashion applicable to his very simple brain hit on the possibility that Mrs. Giles might know where the etching was. Astoundingly, it seemed, he had been right.

Again, the priceless plates. Once they were in Wade's hands he could light out with them and reap, as he saw it and as it, in fact, was, a fortune larger than his dreams. But Smith had come back, and Wade's moronically packed luggage had put Smith wise.

Mrs. Giles would wonder, Parling said, how it was that he should have decided not to go to the plant tonight. How he happened to have been on hand when Smith left the house and so was able to tail him. Well, it was because of her.

(They *must* do something for that Mr. Smith and Mr. Wade. They hadn't moved. It was so kind of Mr. Parling to tell her all these things, but surely the tale could be delayed until later?)

"You see," Parling said, "I followed your taxi from Merkwin's Emporium this afternoon. I saw your most curious interest in the close vicinity of the shack which Smith and Wade had occupied. I didn't and I don't know what your interest was. It doesn't matter. But I knew you were onto something and I was afraid.

"I was afraid, Mrs. Giles, that you would talk to Smith. You would have tipped my hand before I got the invaluable plates. You would have driven him to flight. And so I did not leave the grounds."

Parling, with the faintest of sighs, relaxed. Well, he had lulled her now. He had done what he could. He took out a cigar and clipped off its end.

His voice was businesslike.

"If you will get the plates for me, Mrs. Giles, I will phone Washington that the case is closed."

The fleck of gold. Banding the cigar. In bright sunlight of the morning when she had driven home with Kent from the station and had met Mr. Parling standing on the porch. The cigar in his mouth. The flash, in a ray of sunlight, of its band of gold. Then in the drawing room, in its partial shade, the duller gleam of a band when he had smoked again.

As he had smoked when he had stood near the shack and talked with Russdorff while Hopkins had watched them from the box. (*As to who this rival mob leader was, frankly he didn't know.*) Liar. He knew too well. It was himself.

Mrs. Giles knew what she was in for. What Kent and Hopkins and Ella and Leila, what all of them were in for. Mr. Parling would kill the lot of them, one of those terrifying endings of Shakespeare's, where the curtain would fall on a tableau of corpses.

Parling's voice took on an impatient edge.

"Get them, Mrs. Giles."

Her blood was ice, but her courage never failed her.

"Mr. Parling, will you let me see your badge?"

His skin grew a little pale. Strangely, he was sorry.

"So you didn't fall for it."

His eyes casually traversed the bright large room. He caught, as they reached the cupboards which lined the eastern wall, the manner in which her muscles tensed.

"So they're in one of those," he said.

He did not have to tell her what he meant. He took the revolver with its silencer again from his pocket and held it negligently as he backed toward the eastern wall, facing her, watching her, ready to stifle a scream with the revolver's gentle, deadly *phutt*!

And after her (she felt this like a dagger in her heart) he might kill Kent. His hand, she saw, was ready for the knob of the first cupboard door. This was the one in which she had always hung her smocks. But he would try them all. All of the doors until, with the third, he would come upon Leila's cache. While he opened the door his eyes were still on her: wary, like a beast's eyes sullenly watchful.

Which was why she, and not Mr. Parling, saw, standing in the cupboard among her smocks, Miss Ashley. Her brain could stand no more.

Effacing even her terror and all else, the appalling outrage crashed against Mrs. Giles in a blinding flare: My home, this house which Papa built, is full of *crooks*.

CHAPTER 35

Miss Ashley took a short swing and brought the wrench belonging to the hand press squarely down on Mr. Parling's head.

The carnage was complete.

She stepped from the cupboard. She assured herself that Mr. Parling, now horizontal, was satisfactorily out. She approached the chair where Mrs. Giles, still spellbound, sat. *Was*, Mrs. Giles was wondering, the carnage truly complete?

"Is there an extension phone up here?" Miss Ashley asked.

Mrs. Giles gestured febrilely toward a corner of the room. She watched Miss Ashley move to it and heard her put through a call to Mr. Stedman. What was wrong? Of course: the swivel was no longer in Miss Ashley's walk. And her voice, too, seemed to have changed. As she spoke with Mr. Stedman it could be anybody's.

Miss Ashley hung up and then drew a chair close to Mrs. Giles and sat down. She rested the monkey wrench on her lap.

"There's no necessity of your staying up here, Mrs. Giles," she said in this newly pleasant voice of hers. "I'll watch these three thugs until the police get here."

The voice, the girl's completely altered manner only clouded further Mrs. Giles's dither of confusion. Miss Ashley reminded her so strongly now of any number of the girls who had been her schoolmates at Miss Davidge's and, later, at Vassar.

She said impulsively: "Are you Vassar?"

"Yes, Mrs. Giles—'42."

Then everything was all right.

Everything.

"My dear Effie, I wouldn't dream of leaving you alone here with these three criminal characters. Do you think Joel should join us until Mr. Stedman gets here?"

Miss Ashley hefted the wrench.

"We won't need him," she said.

"Do tell me instantly, dear, just where and when you met Kent."

The story was reasonably simple. As with so many of the young women in her Cleveland crowd, Effie Ashley had wanted to go into war work of a useful nature. She had purposely chosen a factory town away from home so that her normal social life in Cleveland would not impede her.

One day in the Collins plant cafeteria she had overheard a remark made by Wade to Smith (she had not known their names at the time) which had nudged her suspicions.

"The thought of sabotage is always on a worker's mind, Mrs. Giles. Especially in a plant which manufactures explosives."

"My dear child, I can well imagine. I can simply say I shudder."

The remark had not been definite enough to turn in as a report, but it had worried Effie, and she had made it her business to follow the two men up. She located the shack where they lived and, standing outside its paper-thin walls one evening, she had caught further remarks made by Wade. His voice had been so loud that Smith had told him to keep quiet, but Effie by then had heard enough.

It wasn't sabotage. It was counterfeiting, as Mrs. Giles now knew. At the moment it was still pretty vague to Effie, but the implications had struck her as more ominous than ever. This had been on Saturday evening, and she had returned to the vicinity of the shack on Sunday, hoping to be able to find some moment when both men would be out and she could search it.

Smith had come out during the afternoon, leaving Wade behind. Effie had followed Smith and had landed with him at the bond sale. She had overheard the triple chitchat among Dawn Davis, Smith, and Mrs. Giles. She had absorbed the news concerning Kent's possible leave and the renting of River Rest's rooms. She had flown out to get one, her plan being to go into a vampire act and lure the complete dope out of Wade.

"You were perfect, dear," Mrs. Giles said. "You reminded me instantly of that splendid actress, Jeanne Eagels. I could cheerfully have strangled you."

As for her meeting with Kent on the gravel drive, that had been the simplest of all. Effie's uncle—her mother's brother—held a quite important post in Washington.

Mrs. Giles, when she heard the man's name, was profoundly impressed.

"Why, he's practically," she said, "the Merlin of the palace guard."

Effie smiled.

"I know. I called him up from the corner drugstore near Mrs. Aldershot's. He always knows about everything that ever goes on. He knew that Kent was already in Washington and was planning on reaching Bridgehaven the next day."

He had been considerably impressed by Effie's notions and agreed to get in touch with Kent and ship him on that evening by plane, with rendezvous arranged for in the drive, a locale which Effie could keep under comfortable observation from a drawing-room window.

Her idea had been that Kent, knowing the house, would facilitate any search for material which the conspirators might conceal. They had made such a search last night when they had returned to the house instead of going on to a night club.

"Kent and I had been talking out on the drive for about a quarter of an hour, Mrs. Giles, when Russdorff came along."

Russdorff was already stabbed. He had scuffled along the gravel drive and had clutched, in his final agony, at Kent. That was how he had ripped the bracelet and identification tag from Kent's wrist before collapsing back among the shrubbery. In death.

Effie had remembered Russdorff's face. She had seen him talking with Smith and Wade before the shack. His death threw her and Kent into panic, and it was she who had planned the moves covering his "arrival" at the station the next morning.

Parling gave a feeble groan. Effie stood up and inspected the three wrecks on the floor.

"Shouldn't we—are you sure they'll last, dear?" Mrs. Giles asked.

Effie sat down again.

"They'll last."

"There are two things I would like to know. Why did you leave Buffalo as a forwarding address with Mrs. Aldershot and why did you tell me your job was at the Merle plant when you are at the Collins one?"

"I get quite a few letters, Mrs. Giles. The stationery—Mother's especially—wasn't the sort my vamp role would be liable to receive. Smith or Wade might have seen them if they were forwarded here."

"Of course. How clever you were, dear."

"As for the Merle business, I didn't want Smith and Wade to know I was in their plant."

There was one final bewilderment which Mrs. Giles wanted cleared up: just how dear Effie happened to be so fortuitously in the cupboard during the dreadful quarter of an hour which Mrs. Giles had just gone through.

It had not been entirely chance. The studio, with its hand press and materials, had struck Effie as a very logical spot for the concealment of the counterfeit plates. She had come back to River Rest through the storm around six o'clock and, as no one had seen her enter the house, she had hung up her raincoat and hat, taken a flashlight, and had gone straight up to the studio.

She had searched for hours until she was exhausted.

She had finally given it up as a bad job and was starting for the stairs when she had seen Mrs. Giles and Wade coming up them. She had run back into the studio and had hidden in the closet, both to avoid being noticed by Wade and to see what would occur. Luckily she had found the hand press's toolbox on the closet floor and, when the going seemed to be getting rough, she had selected the wrench as a weapon.

"Mrs. Giles, *are* the plates behind that etching you were talking about?"

"We shall see."

Mrs. Giles stood up. Her legs were as weak as water, but they carried her determinedly over to Leila's cache, and there the plates were: concealed in the space behind the little stag and the backing of the frame.

Then she saw Mr. Stedman standing in the studio doorway and what seemed like a press of blue uniforms behind him.

Stedman observed the litter.

"Could be a final curtain by Shakespeare," he muttered. He came inside. He looked with respectful suspicion at Mrs. Giles. "Are you responsible for this?"

He took Mrs. Giles and Effie downstairs into the drawing room while the rest cleared up: a process which involved three stretchers. He heard their stories. He accepted Mrs. Giles's clues and sent her into a faint blush of pleasure by assuring her that the fleck of gold-faced cigar band would rate during the trial as Exhibit A.

He took charge of the priceless plates. He even arranged that Policewoman Jones would stay with Kent until Dr. Hesley could get a real nurse, if Kent should longer need one.

Finally they were gone: Mr. Stedman, the three casualties, and all the law's representatives.

Mrs. Giles locked up. She saw dear Effie to her room and fondly kissed her good night. She stopped in to take a look at Kent: how secure he seemed in his deep, peaceful sleep.

Truly so, at last.

She went to her room and undressed. She took two of Dr. Hesley's pills. She thought, as sleep clutched her, how wonderfully right the house felt again.

Bright sunlight poured through the bedroom windows when she wakened. A clock struck eleven. She lingered awhile on the pillows and enjoyed the sun's warm gold. She permitted herself to dream.

Kent and Effie were at the end of the dream, and possibly it wouldn't be so far off after all. She had the feeling that it wouldn't be. Even Papa would be pleased. She decided just to slip on a dressing gown and run in and see whether Kent was awake. With what a safe feeling she could do so now!

Mrs. Giles got out of bed with joy.

Another day.

ABOUT RUFUS KING

Rufus King (1893–1966) was an American author of Whodunit crime novels. He created four series of detective stories: the first one with Reginald De Puyster, a sophisticated detective similar to Philo Vance; the second one with his more famous character, Lieutenant Valcour; Colin Starr, who appeared in four stories in the *Strand Magazine* during 1940/41; and Detective Bill Duggan, who appeared in three stories in 1956/57. The Bill Duggan stories include his most famous short work, "Malice in Wonderland" (which loaned its title to his 1958 hardcover short story collection).

Modern critics are rediscovering Rufus King's work. Mike Grost, on *Golden Age Detective*, features a long writeup of King, stating: "King had a vivid writing style, with colorful characters, events, and images. He was clearly a born writer."

www.ingramcontent.com/pod-product-compliance
Lightning Source LLC
Chambersburg PA
CBHW020142180626
46810CB00004B/1694